Harlequin Reader Service

CELEBRATES ITS TENTH ANNIVERSARY

An anniversary in the life of a marriage or a business should not go unacknowledged. In business it is a time to reflect on the venture's origins and philosophies, and on the people who have guided it to success. This year Harlequin Reader Service proudly celebrates ten years of service, and to mark the occasion we take great pleasure in presenting to you, our customers, this enchanting book of romantic short stories, in appreciation of your continued support.

The stories in this book represent the best short romance fiction available anywhere and have been specially selected for you, the Harlequin reader. This memento is one we hope you will keep and cherish.

From humble beginnings in 1970, Harlequin Reader Service has grown incredibly and now serves readers from Florida to British Columbia, from Newfoundland to California. Our policy was, and continues to be, to provide a fast, reliable supply of Harlequin books to our readers. As well, we offer those hard-to-find titles not readily available in stores, and special volumes, tailored to our readers' tastes.

Thank you for your warm response to our efforts over the past ten years, and for having made this anniversary a particularly happy and rewarding one.

Harlequin Books

TORONTO • LONDON • LOS ANGELES • AMSTERDAM
SYDNEY • HAMBURG • PARIS • STOCKHOLM • ATHENS • TOKYO

HARLEQUIN'S ROMANTIC SHORT STORIES

Cover illustration by Len Goldberg
Story illustrations by Muriel Wood

ISBN 0-373-82000-3

Printed in Canada

Contents

Return to Meronfield *by Barbara Bennett* 7
Good Things Don't Happen by Mistake *by Suzanne Ebel* 17
James *by Thea Ride* 26
Let Me Count the Ways *by Patricia Condon* 37
I'll Never Fall in Love Again *by Catherine Shaw* 50
Such a Romantic Affair *by Audrie Manley-Tucker* 61
Everything Comes to She Who Waits *by Susan Craig* 74
The Tudor Take-Away *by Pat Lacey* 83
A Donkey Called Delphinia *by Janice Gray* 95
Honey for Tea *by Audrie Manley-Tucker* 105
Summer with Meriel *by Frances Melvin* 117

BARBARA BENNETT

Return to Meronfield

Meronfield was a place to be avoided at all costs, but when the dashboard warning light showed Debbie that her car was overheating, she crawled off the highway at the nearest exit and with a sense of inevitability came back to the village she had last seen eight years ago.

Sam Thorley's garage hadn't changed—the windows of his little office still displayed a collage of ancient, sun-bleached posters, it still sold paraffin, firewood and fresh-laid eggs. Only now it was Sam's son who came out, raising his eyebrows inquiringly. He didn't recognize her, but then, she thought, why should he? Unlike places, people do change, especially eighteen-year-old girls.

"I'll take it around to the back," Jack Thorley said when she explained the trouble, "but there could be a number of things wrong. I'm rather busy and can't promise anything before tomorrow afternoon."

Debbie bit her lip. Tomorrow afternoon—so no date with Miles tonight after all. She didn't know whether to be pleased or sorry.

During the two years she'd known him he had often said such things as, "Have you ever thought how much traveling time, not to mention gas, we'd save if we were together?" Or, "We're both responsible adults and we love each other. Isn't that enough?" Once, when she'd stood by the window of his apartment window admiring the view over the park, he had come to stand behind her. "Why not share it with me?" he had said, but gently, a suggestion rather than a proposition, as if making it easy for her to refuse without embarrassment.

There had been times when she was tempted to say yes. "I need you, Debbie," he told her, "and that's the truth."

"You must remember I've had a very conventional upbringing," she'd said cheerfully. But secretly she knew the real reason for not committing herself; even after eight years the flavor of an old, sweet, crazy relationship lingered.

"One day," Miles had remarked wryly, "I shall have to put aside my principles and ask you to marry me." There had been a faint question in his voice.

But she hadn't answered it. "Yes, one day. But not just yet."

Now, intuitively, she sensed that this evening was the occasion, and here she was in Meronfield—relieved? Disappointed? She didn't know which. And, the small inner voice prompted, wasn't that answer enough?

"Is there anywhere I can get supper and a bed for the night?" she asked Jack Thorley.

"There's the Copper Kettle at the corner of Sheep Lane. You'll get supper there, if nothing else. Turn left at—"

"It's all right. I know it. Surely Miss Croasdale isn't still there? She must be more than seventy now, if I remember right."

"Ah," he said, his face puzzled. "I reckoned you looked familiar. Can't place you, though."

"Debbie Peterson," she said.

"That's it. I remember now." He wiped his hands on a rag. "Well, that's a coincidence. End House is up for auction tomorrow. Isn't that where you used to live with your aunt? And David Verney's coming over from Kingstanton to sell it. He was a great pal of yours. . . ."

To hear the name spoken aloud after so long gave her an unwelcome, tingling shock. "Oh. Yes, it certainly is a coincidence. Well, I'll call in tomorrow about the car. I'll just get my case from the trunk."

Two hours later she was being shown into the front bedroom over the Copper Kettle tea shop.

Miss Croasdale, kindly and garrulous, had been sympathetic. "My dear, if your car's not ready then you're very welcome to the spare room here. I'm on my own, and it will be nice to have company." Then she echoed Jack Thorley's words. "You know, it's a remarkable coincidence, but guess who called in to see me this morning? David Verney." She leaned back as if waiting for the impact of her words. "Such a nice young man, and done well, too. He's a partner in a firm of auctioneers over in Kingstanton. Do you remember those Saturday mornings when you both used to come to eat my Shrewsbury biscuits, still warm from the oven?" She smiled reminiscently. "Such a lively pair you were. You've changed, but that's to be expected. You're thinner and quite elegant. Citified, you might say."

"Well, those Saturday mornings were a long time ago." Debbie smiled and turned to hang the jacket of her cream flannel suit over the back of a cane-bottomed chair. "You look the same though. Meronfield seems to have the effect of preserving everything. . . ."

And there lay in the crux of the matter the certainty that her feelings for David were preserved. Then what kind of future could she share with Miles, she wondered bleakly. "I'm so grateful to you for putting me up for the night," she resumed, to cover her distraction. "I was on my way back to London after a friend's wedding."

Miss Croasdale nodded wistfully. "I do like a nice wedding. I used to think that you and David might . . . . Still, you were very young then. It's funny to think that he's been here today, and now you're here."

Yes, the inner voice said. *Funny. Especially since you could have left your car and caught the London train. So why are you here? So that you can see David again and remember? So that you can hope?*

It felt strange to be walking along the little High street after so many years. Here she had walked with David; there was the tiny garden behind the war memorial where they'd sat holding hands and talking. How they'd talked! And the shabby little tennis court where they'd played on summer evenings; the Institute Hall where they'd danced on Saturday nights, deriding the naiveté of the music as if they hadn't dared admit to enjoying themselves. They'd made a point of denigrating Meronfield as if its amenities fell far below their enlightened needs.

The telephone booth near the bus shelter was surprisingly clean and unvandalized. One rainy night David had pulled her in here and kissed her, and now she stood inside recalling their closeness. Her back had been pressed against the coin box and she'd wanted to move, yet wanted not to move . . . ever. Now, rebuking herself, she dialed Miles's number with firm, businesslike fingers.

"You're where?" he said. "Meronfield? Your car—oh, bad luck. Still, it can't be helped. I'm sorry about tonight, though. I'd better cancel the table. Yes, sure, I'll call your office and explain. How was the wedding?"

"Lovely. Miles, I haven't any more change. . . ."

"See you tomorrow then. I've missed you."

As she came out of the booth she wished, perversely, that he had shown more disappointment, even anger at the cancellation of their date, then she reproved herself. Miles's equanimity, his consistent good-natured acceptance of the unavoidable, were two of his most endearing traits.

She knew that she'd go to the auction tomorrow. She'd be pulled there to see David as he was now. Trying to escape memories was useless. In London she could almost succeed in burying them beneath the demands of an interesting job and her relationship with Miles. But she wasn't in London now. She was here, where all her memories began.

Meronfield seemed to have closed its doors, as if television had imposed a curfew upon the village. She walked slowly past David's old home toward the end of the street where the hills rose to shoulder each other gently. Sheep scattered the slopes like dandelion clocks, and a slow feather of smoke rose from an isolated chimney. Hedgerows were blurred with the ivy growth of years, and the setting sun drew to the west the evening's clouds. It might have been an illustration for a health-food package. And there on the left was the crooked ridge of End House.

Despite her rejection of this place, the thin needle of nostalgia pricked painfully. She had lived here for almost eighteen years, ever since her parents died in a car crash and her mother's sister had made a home for her. Now the notice of tomorrow's auction leaned askew over the white gate, and she wondered who would come to live in the rooms that she had once shared with Aunt Molly. Doubtless someone was prepared to pay a good price for a house that could boast original seventeenth-century paneling and graffiti by Cromwell's Ironsides.

She recalled her aunt's perturbed listening face during autumn evenings. "The wind's rising," she would say. "That will probably mean a few loose tiles tomorrow." Or, "There's a damp patch on the dining-room wall. I expect it's that downspout again."

"Why don't you sell it?" Debbie had asked with the confident wisdom of youth. "Buy somewhere modern?"

"But I couldn't do that, dear." Her aunt's face had been shocked. "My family have lived here for four generations. I wouldn't settle anywhere else."

"Oh, settle," Debbie had said disparagingly. "Everyone here is so settled." Everyone except herself and David. He had just acquired a noisy old sports car. They had roared around the countryside to drink half-pint shandies in village pubs. To both of them life was a series of open doors that led out of Meronfield, even if only to a similar village. But the illusion was there—they were getting away, going places together.

Always together. Until early one evening when David parked the car at the top of a hill and they sat gazing down on Meronfield. "Look at it," he had said. "The petrified village. We could be frozen there forever. Yet the world is waiting outside. It's all there, and who can we blame but ourselves if we don't accept its invitation? Well, I've made up my mind. I'll have a couple of years traveling, just knocking around, earning my keep and seeing places."

She had shivered with delight at the prospect and waited for him to say, with that challenging lift of his dark eyebrows, "Coming with me?" Somehow she must persuade Aunt Molly to let her go. But David was silent, his eyes narrowed against the slanting rays of the sun so that his short black lashes looked thicker than ever. With a slow desolation she knew that he was contemplating a future in which she had no part. "No strings," they had told each other earlier, because it seemed a worldly-wise attitude to take, but now the absence of strings cut painfully.

"Where will you go?" she had said at last, staring out over the passenger door so that he should not see her face.

"Who knows? That's not the important part. It's the going that matters. But—" he shrugged "—Anatolia, Tibet, the golden road to Samarkand."

She'd wanted to cry, "Take me with you."

But he was dissociating himself even further, saying, "And how about you, Debbie? What are you going to do? I know—you'll stay here, gradually fossilizing." He had made spooky movements with his hands, but she hadn't laughed.

"I won't." She spoke hotly, saying the first thing that came to mind, the obvious thing. "I'll go to London, find a job and an apartment. There'll be—oh, concerts, the theater, exhibitions, interesting people. . . ."

And that was how it had been, how it had to be so that memories could be kept at arm's length, except at those traitorous moments when a tune or even a trick of the evening light caught her unawares and told her that she had forgotten nothing.

She had returned to Meronfield four months later for Aunt Molly's funeral. By that time David's parents had moved away, and afterward there had been no reason to come back. Until now.

The gate of End House stood ajar and she closed it carefully, as she had done years ago to keep stray dogs off her aunt's garden. Then, suddenly, she swung it open and walked slowly up the path toward the house. Patches of brighter orange, like random mosaic, showed where some of the old tiles had been replaced. The downspouts were of black plastic now, and apparently efficient. Judging by the sparkling paintwork, its late owners had cared for End House. She felt a soft gratitude on Aunt Molly's behalf. It was all so very much neater than it had been. She should have experienced a sense of homecoming, yet she did not. That, perhaps, was the saddest part of all.

She rounded the corner of the outer wall and jumped as a voice behind her said, "Can I help you?" Then, "No . . . Debbie? It can't be."

"But it is." Was the knocking of her heart only the rhythm of shock? "David. I didn't expect to see you here."

"I could say the same." He was watching her; she saw his gaze move over her hair with its reddish highlights more apparent than when they'd met, over her simple, expensive suit standing out against the somber background of the yews that rustled in the wind. "Actually," he said absently,

"I'm selling it tomorrow. It's all there on the sign." He moved his head slightly, indicating. "I came over to satisfy myself on a couple of points. But you . . . you could be a beautiful ghost."

She smiled, acknowledging the compliment. "I was on my way back to town after a wedding when my car started to misbehave. I've left it with Jack Thorley, and I'm staying with Miss Croasdale. So what you see is the real me."

"That one and only you. And believe me, it's good to see you again. You've changed quite a bit." They stood wordlessly for a moment, then he said, "Would you like to take a final look before it comes under the hammer? Besides, the midges are biting."

She laughed, breaking the spell, and followed him into the flagged hall, cool and dim as it had always been on summer evenings. Apart from the modernized kitchen, a second bathroom, and radiators everywhere, little had changed. She almost expected Aunt Molly to come peering out of the room saying anxiously, "Is that you, Debbie?" as if visitors had been frequent.

"Mind the step," David said, and reached for her hand. "We've got such a lot to talk about. What unbelievable luck that our paths should cross again!"

She didn't know what to say, and that was strange because once there had never been time to say all that had to be said. She sought for something and finally asked, "Speaking of paths, did you ever find it—the golden road to Samarkand?"

He looked puzzled, as if he'd forgotten. "Is that where I was going?" Then he laughed. "It must have been just a figure of speech, I suppose."

He had changed, too, she decided. He still had that free, fresh-air look, but he was more substantial now, more real and confident.

"I got as far as Naples and discovered that I had roots. They began to tug. Oh, not just this place, but . . . well, order, a program, ambition, I suppose. Freedom was fine at first, but it palled because there was too much of it. So I came back and found a job and worked hard and qualified. So here I am. It probably sounds less glamorous than the golden road, but that was just kid's stuff."

"Weren't you sorry? I mean that it turned out to be just a dream?" she asked curiously.

"Why should I be? It showed me what I really wanted. There was one thing I was sorry about, though." He drew her hand through his arm. "You. Losing you. Lord, I must have been arrogant."

"Yes, you were a little. So was I, I suppose. How lofty and patronizing we were about this place."

"Well, I suppose we enjoyed knocking it. It was part of the game." He took out a handkerchief and flapped it over the broad window seat. They sat, his shoulder companionably solid against hers, and their reminiscences held them in a delicate web for a while. "I hoped that you'd still be here when I got back. But it seemed that you'd vanished without a trace. Well now, how is London? Did it give you whatever it was that you wanted?"

She realized with a shock that he hadn't even remembered what it was that she'd wanted, whereas she had remembered everything. "Yes, it did. I'm assistant to a public relations officer in a large hotel." She told him a little about her life.

"It sounds great. No humdrum nine-to-five job for you. You sound quite settled."

She nodded, thinking how strange it was that he'd used that word—their earlier indictment against life in Meronfield. "Yes, I believe I am," she said, faintly surprised to be putting it into such words.

He lifted her hand. "And you're not married."

"No. I was never quite sure enough. And you?"

He shook his head. They sat for a time as the twilight thickened and their features blurred into pale shapes. She turned to look out over the garden, and it was the most natural thing in the world that he, too, should turn at that moment and kiss her. She waited for the old wonder, the realization that she had, in all respects, come home now, the conviction that once they'd got past the preliminary stages of picking up the threads their relationship would go on. But there was nothing, only the poignant atmosphere of departure in an empty house. And oddly, she felt a wild, surging relief.

Gently she pulled away. "I have to go."

"But you'll be back."

"No," she said softly. "I don't belong here anymore. Once, perhaps, but we've both moved on. You said something about roots, and I have them, too, but I've discovered that they're not where I thought. Well—" suddenly she lifted her face and kissed his cheek "—good luck, David, with everything. And goodbye."

"Can't I persuade you to come up sometime? No—" he sighed "—I can't. There's nothing more final than a kiss like that."

"Perhaps the end was long ago and we didn't realize."

"Something remained though."

"Memories," she said. "That's all."

Miles sounded surprised to hear her voice again. "I thought you'd run out of coins," he said practically.

"I changed a bill."

"That's my girl. I wondered what had happened to your usual resourcefulness. And did you know you could have caught a train back? I looked up the times after you'd telephoned. You had me worried, darling. I was forced to the conclusion that you were ducking out of tonight's date."

His voice was, as always, laconic, but now she sensed that this was a protection, sensed that he was protecting her, too, by making it easy for her to answer in a similar vein—as she always had in the past. Now, however, she said seriously, "Perhaps you were right."

She heard the self-derisory smile in his voice. "Well, I can't truthfully say that your trepidation was unfounded. I've tried leading you into marriage gently—thought that if we were together then you'd soon see that marriage was the natural progression for us. That didn't work, so—but you spiked my guns by not coming back. And I had it all prepared—a secluded table at the Silver Pheasant, your favorite flowers waiting there, even champagne on ice. I was going to make it so darned hard for you to refuse."

"Miles, I was going to say that. . . ."

"I love you, Debbie." His voice hardened, grew vehement, and she had to hold the receiver away from her ear. "Damn it, do you hear me? I've told you before but you weren't listening. I had the strange feeling that you were hearing something else, even someone else. . . ."

"Miles, listen to me. I don't know how to say it. I'm not even really used to the idea yet, but I have the feeling that things are already . . . well, settled. I didn't see it before but now it seems just a question of—"

"Putting it in writing?" he said wonderingly. "Do you really mean that?"

"That's exactly what I mean."

There was silence, but despite the miles of cable between them, she felt very close to him. "Darling," he said gently, after a while, "something's happened in the last couple of hours. Shouldn't I know about it? Especially since you've told me that nothing ever happens in Meronfield?"

She thought of all the analogies she might use—she could tell him that some roots flourished more vigorously if transplanted; tell him that what she'd seen as an escape route was, in reality, the "golden road". She realized that she was echoing David, but that didn't matter now, and after all, David had played a small but important part in this moment. Oh, there were all kinds of things she might have said, but she could only whisper, "Yes, something happened. I love you so much. And I don't need favorite flowers on secluded tables and champagne in ice buckets. Just you, Miles, and I'll be home tomorrow."

SUZANNE EBEL

Good Things Don't Happen by Mistake

Daisy's roommate, Sarah, was rather heavy on the subject of the coming interview. They had finished supper and Sarah, sipping coffee, was looking with approval at the flowers in the window box (all her own work).

"You realize Aubrey Foster is the managing director of the firm," said Sarah—not for the first time. "One can't go higher than that."

Sarah was in business, and Daisy had often noticed how the names of directors, chairmen, people like that, came into the conversation. Rather like a practised skier mentions mountains. But Sarah had a kind heart and was wonderfully efficient.

"When I called he said he'd be delighted to see you, Daisy. It looks like a good chance this time," added Sarah.

Sarah was small, dark, dressed with style and practical. Daisy was willowy, blond, with a snub nose and a habit of scribbling poetry. The differences between the girls suited them. Sarah liked Daisy's unexpectedness—she even liked some of the poems. Daisy liked Sarah's strength and common sense, and passionately admired Sarah's way with her boyfriend, John.

"You're so lucky to be in love!" Daisy would wail. "I never have been."

"It'll happen. It'll happen," was the positive reply.

Daisy wasn't too sure. She only seemed to meet fellows who wanted to borrow records or money. Or have their jeans patched.

"It's your own fault. Hide the albums," said Sarah.

There were times when Sarah had fits of trying to organize Daisy; at present it was the problem of a job. Daisy, she declared, had been waitressing long enough. She must make the effort. "I thought you wanted to go into publishing."

"Oh, I do. More than anything."

"What have you done about it?"

"I've tried. Truly."

"Months ago. Now what one needs is an introduction," Sarah mused. "Let me see . . . who—why, of course! Aubrey Foster!"

She'd actually telephoned right away, spoken to this exalted character and arranged an appointment.

"But how do you know he wants to see me?" asked Daisy.

"Daisy, higher-ups in business *have* to see new people. They can't afford to miss the chance of finding someone clever."

"But—"

"And you've no idea whether you are clever or not," interrupted Sarah severely.

The morning of the interview it was raining steadily. A soft, muddy kind of day. When Daisy, who'd swopped days off with another waitress, wandered into the kitchen, she found Sarah dressed for work in blue and green and looking particularly perfect. Breakfast was ready.

"An egg?" said Daisy, surprised.

"You have to be at your best for the interview."

"Oh, Sarah. Thanks. But I'm not nervous."

"Good things don't happen by mistake," said Sarah, expertly making coffee. I've been trying to think of anything that might help. And while I was having my bath I suddenly remembered something. My boss said it once—that at an interview one should always let the prospective boss do the talking and just listen intelligently. The less *you* say the better. Sounds odd, but he swore it works."

"Okay. I shall quite like saying nothing," said Daisy, loyally plowing through the egg.

"Ah. But remember there are *ways* of saying nothing."

Just before leaving, Sarah peered around Daisy's door. "What are you wearing?"

"My black cord. Why?"

They both knew Daisy had been tempted to wear her

white dungarees. Sarah pretended she'd thought of no such thing, waved her goodbye and wished her luck.

"Don't talk too much!"

Daisy dressed slowly. *You'd think I never stopped chattering,* she thought, pulling on a white sweater and zipping up her black corduroy skirt. She looked out the window. The soft rain pattered down, so she put on an old raincoat that always reminded her of Bogart and borrowed Sarah's second umbrella.

On the long bus journey she felt cheerful. Waitressing was all very well, but it was true that she did long, and had indeed tried now and then, to be in publishing. Why did people always say "in"? As if one had to jump into a lake? Or the sea, perhaps?

She thought dreamily about publishing. Bright-jacketed books. Authors writing masterpieces in Highland cottages. Artists painting book jackets.

She was in good time as she stepped down from the bus and walked toward a mostly glass block that towered over the rest of the buildings. *Somewhere up there,* thought Daisy, looking at indistinguishable windows, *is Mr. Aubrey Foster, Managing Director. One can't go higher than that.*

The doorman was helpful. "There's another entrance at the end of the alleyway on the right. Double doors."

Daisy went down a narrow paved alley. There were the doors. A large notice said, Use Next Door Please! She popped obediently through the next door, asked the elevator operator for Mr. Foster, and was wafted upward.

The receptionist, a plump, dark lady, was knitting a green sweater and wearing an identical pink one. She looked surprised when Daisy asked for Mr. Foster.

"I have an appointment. Eleven-thirty."

"Mr. Foster. I really am sorry. I'm afraid he's in Amsterdam.

Daisy gasped. How often had Sarah extolled the marvelous efficiency, the reliability, like steel, of the higher-ups.

"Mr. Powell is taking interviews this morning," said the plump receptionist. "I'll buzz him."

"Here's my name and address," said Daisy helpfully.

The receptionist dialed on the intercom. "Mr. Powell? Reception here. I have a—" looking at Daisy's note "—Miss Daisy Elizabeth Morris here. Appointment with Mr. Foster. Could you . . .?"

She hung up. "Mr. Powell is just coming," she said, and returned with some relief to the green knitting.

A young man came briskly down the corridor. He was tall, redheaded, with a tough, freckled face.

"Miss Morris? Hello. Come in, would you?"

He bustled her into a large, plain office with large windows overlooking wet rooftops and a church spire or two. She was settled into a chair facing his desk, and offered coffee. "From the machine and pretty horrible. But hot," he said.

While they waited for the coffee, he apologized for Mr. Foster's absence. "You know how it is with trips abroad."

Daisy untruthfully said she did.

He asked her when she had graduated and what she was doing now. When Daisy explained about the waitressing, he looked impressed. "A hardy girl," he said. They both smiled.

Her spirits rose a little. She did like the man on the other side of the desk; the fact that he wasn't—after all—a higher-up was rather comfortable. She could imagine him with authors . . . a budding Evelyn Waugh, for instance. But his office was a disappointment—not a book in sight. Daisy had thought there would be rainbows of them.

"Shall we talk a bit about the job, Miss Morris?"

Daisy nodded seriously and settled down to take Sarah's advice. She fixed her brown eyes on the young man with concentrated attention.

"The first thing to mention, of course, is the traveling. There's a great deal of it," said Nick Powell.

What?

But she said nothing. She listened.

"That's the basic trouble with this kind of work," he went on thoughtfully. "It's a wonderful training for the future, of course. But one has no home life. I know I didn't. Three or four days in each city—a week or ten days at the outside. Moving about all the time. It isn't easy to live like that."

"I suppose not," muttered Daisy.

She was totally and completed confused. What on earth could this publishing job be? What had Sarah said to Mr. Aubrey Foster? Sarah was rather daring in business—had she indicated that Daisy might actually be turned into a book saleswoman? Daisy knew perfectly well she'd never have the nerve.

"I'm afraid," went on Nick Powell easily, with his warm smile, "there's another problem one has to consider. You'll have a senior with you, naturally. But different firms often use entirely different systems."

"I suppose they must," said poor Daisy.

"That's what makes it such fascinating work, but also makes it tough. Doing a firm's audit is often like starting an entirely fresh job every time."

Daisy's eyes nearly popped out of her head.

She was in the wrong place!

But it's impossible, she thought desperately, no longer listening to Nick Powell's voice. *There can't be two Mr. Fosters. But there are. There must be.*

Nick Powell continued his improbable description of the work of a traveling auditor. He spoke of schedules, double entries, books—ah, what different books those were—computer data and systems. *How can I jump up and say I'm not what he thinks,* thought Daisy, getting more frantic. *He'll think I'm mad—but I'm not! The doorman sent me here. Oh, help.*

"I think that pretty well covers everything, Miss Morris," finished Nick Powell. "Naturally you will want to think it over, and perhaps you'd drop a line to Mr. Foster. This is only a preliminary chat, you know. Mr. Foster will want to see you. I'll tell him that we met today."

He stood up and so did Daisy. Now was the time to speak. But he took her hand in a large warm grasp and looked at her with a smile, and she didn't say a word.

Blessedly alone in the downstairs entrance, she stared up at the list of firms.

Little, Foster & Partners, Accountants.

And a minute later, through the first pair of swinging doors—the one without the taped notice actually opened—there it was: Peter Edwards & Aubrey Foster, Publishers.

The clock on the wall said she was forty minutes too late.

Sarah's face was a mask of horror. "You did *what*? You saw *who*?"

"Whom," corrected John, Sarah's boyfried, who was looking rather strange as he listened.

"What job were you interviewed for?" cried Sarah, her voice rising.

"Traveling auditor," said John, and could contain himself no longer. He burst into a shout of laughter.

"Oh, Daisy, Daisy, why didn't you accept? What a whirl you'd be, doing the company's books."

"It is not in the least funny," snapped Sarah. She was extremely cross. "What will Aubrey Foster think? One does not make an appointment for a friend with a managing director and the friend simply does not turn up. It is extremely rude."

"I am sorry, Sarah."

"It wasn't the girl's fault. Two Fosters," said John, who was short and dark and earnestly trying to straighten his face.

"Did you phone and apologize?" demanded Sarah.

"I didn't like to. I thought he'd never believe me."

"Good grief. I'd better do it."

Sarah slammed off to the telephone.

John met Daisy's mournful stare, and began to chuckle again. "Oh, Daisy. Nobody but you could get through the whole interview without talking. Why didn't you say something?"

"At first because Sarah had said the less one talks at interviews, the better. And then.... Then I don't know."

John's eyes had begun to sparkle again, but Sarah marched back and frowned at him. "Mr. Foster was extremely gritty. I don't blame him. I explained what had happened, and he accepted it; but what surprised him was that you hadn't called his secretary afterward. However, he says he will see you tomorrow at twelve. Which is very nice of him."

Daisy said a crushed thank-you. Sarah and John (still none too straight-faced) went off to a disco. As they left the apartment, Daisy heard Sarah say, "It is not funny and stop sniggering."

The apartment was quiet after they'd gone. It had grown dark, and Daisy switched on the lights and changed into her dungarees, which were a comfort in time of trial. She washed her hair.

She was having a gloomy cup of coffee—too dispirited for supper—and listening to a frightening radio play about robots when the front doorbell rang.

"Yes?" she said nervously from the other side of the door.

"It's Nick Powell," called a voice.

Oh, help, thought Daisy.

As she opened the door she blushed a burning scarlet. Even her nose was red.

"Sorry to barge in. Have you got a moment?"

"Yes. Come in."

She led the way to the sitting room in silence loud with embarrassment, and asked him to sit down.

"I found you because Molly, our receptionist, had your address."

"Oh."

He looked at the girl in the white dungarees. She looked distinctly younger, and her long fair hair was damp.

"I felt I had to see you," he said.

"Yes." The blush had faded. She looked at him dolefully.

"I checked after you'd gone," said Nick Powell. "And Mr. Foster had no appointment this morning with a Miss Morris. So then I began thinking about you, and there was something. . . ."

"Not very auditorish?"

"Exactly."

Daisy explained for the second time that evening. She braced herself for the roar of laughter, but he only looked interested.

"Poor you," he said when she finished. "I must say you did look a bit horrified when I was describing the job. I thought it was the idea of traveling. Why didn't you stop me?"

"I don't know," Daisy said, and sighed. "It—well—when you'd taken the trouble to see me and everything, it seemed so rude."

He gave her the oddest look.

They talked a little longer. About auditing. Publishing. Coincidences. Then he said, "Look—have you had supper? Shall we go to that Italian place on Linden Road? I'd like it very much if you'd come."

They had a delicious supper. Daisy felt happy. He was funny and interesting, quick and kind. When he brought her home to the front door, he gave her a hug.

"What time is your appointment with the real Mr. Foster?"

"Twelve tomorrow. Should I have the nerve to go?"

"Of course. And he'll snap you up. We all want to do that."

He hugged her again. He'd call tomorrow evening, he said.

Daisy went to bed in a haze and slept badly. She woke at four and lay thinking about Nick Powell. She slept again and woke feeling distinctly sloppy. It was a surprise to find Sarah getting breakfast and still cross.

It seemed odd, after having been wished a severe good-luck by Sarah, to put on the black corduroy skirt and white sweater and the Bogart raincoat (it was still raining). She took the same bus and walked up to the same glass building. But this time she thought that somewhere among those lines of windows was a young man who had hugged her tightly.

She thought about Nick as she went through the doors and up in the elevator. She got out of the elevator and suddenly, "Daisy!"

It was Nick. She couldn't believe her eyes. He grasped both her hands and gave her the longest, loveliest look.

"I knew you'd come. I've been waiting."

"But—"

"You came to me. You were thinking of me. I've been doing the same. Do you always do such beautiful things? Come on, we have five minutes to get you there."

He rushed her back into the elevator, into the neighboring building.

"I'm delivering you in person this time. I'm not having anyone interview you except this publishing character."

They went up in the elevator holding hands. The elevator stopped, and Nick steered her through more doors. And suddenly she was in a rainbow world. Books of every color spilled along shelves. Display cards showed leaping horses, windmills, girls, tigers.

A middle-aged lady at the reception desk said, "Miss Daisy Morris?"

"Come and pick me up when you're through," said Nick. "I'm taking you to lunch."

Nick always claimed afterward that it was entirely due to him that Mr. Foster gave her a job.

"But, Nick, why? I'd behaved so crazily. I wouldn't have thought bosses liked people to do that."

"Bosses like people who are determined to find them, no matter what," said Nick. There was a little pause. "And you found me, too, didn't you, darling Daisy?"

THEA RIDE

James

James was six feet tall in his socks, broad shouldered and dark haired. He also had the most beautiful smile imaginable. James had charm and a wonderful way with women. Facially, he resembled a cross between Tom Jones and Alan Bates. He was the sort of man any girl would be pleased to be seen with. And as if that wasn't enough, he was extremely nice.

James was born, fully grown, at the age of twenty-six on the seventeenth of March, 1978. He was the brainchild of Carol Valentine.

Carol was twenty-three, five foot three in her stockings, rather bright and extremely pretty, and any man should have been pleased to be seen with her. She felt neither bright nor pretty, however, since Tom Everton had decided not to marry her after all. He was the reason she had come to London. Further than that, we need not discuss Tom Everton; he did not deserve her, anyway.

It was for the benefit of the other girls in the office that Carol invented James. On her arrival in London she had signed on with a temporary-help agency and had taken the first secretarial job offered. She didn't particularly like it, but pounding away at a typewriter day after day was a kind of therapy—Tom Everton had done something destructive to her initiative and she needed time to build it up again. But we are not discussing Tom Everton.

During coffee and lunch breaks, the other girls' conversation concerned their boyfriends or husbands, and Carol used to sit quietly during these sessions feeling distinctly uncomfortable. Myra, who had red hair and freckles and no inhibitions, turned to Carol one day and asked, "What's your boyfriend's name?"

"James," said Carol instantaneously, giving the first name that entered her head. Curious, she thought afterward, that the first name that entered her head was not Tom—curious, and healthy. She must be recovering.

Everyone stopped talking and looked at Carol.

"What does he do?" asked Myra again.

Carol considered. What would James do? "He's in business," she said. "He's a consultant."

"Sounds very serious," someone said.

"Oh, he's not," said Carol, warming to her subject. "Well, he's serious about business, of course, but he's great fun."

"I wish Eddie was," sighed someone else.

Carol's imagination took flight. By the time she had finished describing James and all his glories she had acquired new status in the office and, in a curious way, a new outlook on life.

She thought about James on the bus as she made her way home. She thought how pleasant it would be if, when she arrived at her rather small and dingy bed-sitter, the phone would be ringing and it would be James. "I've got two tickets for the theater tonight, darling. Are you free?" Or maybe he would be waiting on her doorstep with a bunch of roses in one hand and a supermarket bag in the other. "I thought we'd have an evening in tonight. I've a couple of steaks here and a bottle of wine...."

It would be nice, thought Carol.

From the bus she saw hanging in the window of an art shop a paper mobile, consisting of one large bird and several smaller ones floating beneath it. The birds were delicately painted in blue and gold and looked poised to fly away. She disembarked at the next stop and bought the mobile. It cost two and one half pounds, and she had to wait forty-five minutes before an empty bus arrived to complete her journey home, but she hummed as she hung the pretty mobile in her bed-sitter window. The little room took on quite a different quality with these rare and fragile creatures hanging there.

"James gave me those," she imagined herself saying to a visitor. "Well, yes, he is a bit frivolous at times, you know. But awfully reliable."

She boiled an egg, having eaten quite well in the cafeteria at midday, then switched on the radio and pulled out her crocheting. She was making a poncho for herself in blue and gold, like the birds.

In her head, James was saying, "What's a nice girl like you doing all alone this fine evening?"

"Ah," said Carol. "If only you were real."

"I am real, in a sense," said James. " 'If onlys' don't get people very far, though, do they?"

"That's true," said Carol. "I said you had a lot of common sense."

"More than you, if you ask me," said James. "Sitting there moping, with the great big world out there waiting to be explored."

"I'm sitting here because nobody wants me," said Carol, wiping a tear from the corner of her eye.

"If there's one thing I can't stand," said James, "it's self-pity. How can anyone want you if nobody sees you? You have to get out and meet people. Didn't we see something in the paper about a poetry group tonight?"

"Yes, but . . . ."

"No buts. Get the paper."

So she went to the poetry reading, which was held in the upstairs room of a pub, and it turned out to be a lot of fun. Carol found herself talking to her neighbors, and one young man insisted on buying her a drink and walking her home. She felt rather uncertain, but he was very persistent. When, at the front gate, he asked meaningfully if he could come in for coffee, she said she was awfully sorry, but James wouldn't like it. James, she explained, was her boyfriend, who was away on a business trip and was, incidentally, a karate expert. The young man went away.

So James turned out to have more uses than one.

After that, James persuaded Carol to visit the theater and the opera and have supper at the nearby health-food restaurant. Gradually Carol found herself acquiring new friends. But she didn't acquire anyone remotely resembling James.

"If only you were real," she sighed one evening, cutting the last piece of wool from her blue and gold poncho.

James was silent.

"I didn't mean to offend you," said Carol. "I mean, I'm having a very nice time as it is, but . . . ."

"Ifs and buts," said James crossly. "That poncho looks terrific. You have a real feeling for color, you know. Ever thought of taking up painting?"

"Hmm . . ." said Carol thoughtfully. "Well, your suggestions usually turn out pretty well."

So on Saturday afternoon, wearing her blue and gold poncho, she joined an art class at her local adult education institute. Though she felt clumsy and unpracticed, the teacher was encouraging, and afterward, feeling quite buoyant, Carol went into the cafeteria for a coffee.

It was there that she met Lawrence and Tony.

She couldn't help noticing them in the lineup because, while Tony was fair and not very tall, Lawrence was the exact image of James. When they came to sit at Carol's table, she could scarcely take her eyes off him. Even more astonishing, the impact seemed to be mutual. He was staring at her, hard.

"You have some paint on your nose," he said eventually.

Carol blushed and groped in her purse for her compact and a tissue.

"Such a pretty nose, too," he went on, looking at her with those dark, intense eyes she had thought only James possessed.

"No need to guess what class you've been at," his friend remarked laughingly.

The two men, it turned out, were studying Spanish, with a view to summer holidays. They shared an apartment; Lawrence was in advertising and Tony in computers. Carol wished she was involved in something more interesting than office work and decided it was time to look for another job. The conversation flowed, however; both men seemed interested in her, and she blossomed under their attention. Particularly the attention of six-foot, dark-haired Lawrence.

It was odd the way James popped into the discussion, but he had become so much a part of her life that when he crept into the conversation it was almost as if he'd done so on purpose. "When James suggested this folk club the other night . . ." she heard herself saying.

"Who's James?" asked Lawrence, alert.

"Oh, just a friend," she said, looking, she knew, extremely self-conscious.

"Boyfriend?" Lawrence raised an eyebrow.

"Sort of," she said.

"Engaged?"

"No . . . not exactly."

He relaxed and smiled. Carol relaxed, too. He was amazingly attractive, she thought. And charming, and attentive, and all the things James would have been . . . if he'd been real.

When Lawrence asked her if she would like to join them for a meal, she accepted as if hypnotized. She was a little annoyed at being asked to join them rather than just him, but Tony was pleasant enough and friendly. Also, he owned a car and Lawrence didn't, which was useful when it came time to go home. The three of them—four, counting James—had a thoroughly enjoyable evening.

"See you again soon?" Lawrence asked, holding her hand at the door.

"It depends a little bit on James . . ." she found herself saying, and wondered why on earth she'd said that when what she'd meant was, *oh, yes, as soon as possible*.

When she was alone, she asked, "Why did you make me say that?"

"No harm in playing a little hard to get," replied James.

"But I don't need to play games," she said. "Not with him, not with Lawrence. Oh, James, I think I'm in love. I'm sure I'm in love."

"You were sure you were in love with Tom Everton," said James.

"Oh, him. Let's not discuss him. I don't want to think about him anymore."

"But maybe you should," said James.

"What do you mean?"

James was silent.

"Well, I don't need you anyway," said Carol crossly. "Not now when I've found the real thing."

"I think I'll stick around a bit longer," said James perversely. "Just in case."

Carol's doorbell rang unexpectedly the next morning, which was Sunday. She was wearing her new long flowered cotton skirt, just in case the doorbell should ring unexpectedly.

The unexpected person, however, was not Lawrence but Tony. She tried not to let her face drop.

"I was just passing," he said, smiling. "Wondered if you'd offer me a cup of coffee?"

"Sure." With as good a grace as possible, Carol put the kettle on and spooned instant coffee into two mugs.

"How's Lawrence today?" she asked brightly as she poured, knowing she hadn't a hope of sounding casual.

"Oh, he's gone out for the day. To see his mother," he said.

"Oh."

"I was wondering . . . would you like to come out for a while? Take a trip down Regent's Park Canal, maybe?"

For all his cheerful appearance, he sounded very tentative. Carol liked men with assurance, like Lawrence and James, but there was something rather touching about Tony's hesitance. Almost as if he expected her to say no.

"Why not?" whispered James.

"Why not?" echoed Carol. She might as well—she was dressed for it and the sun was shining.

They took a barge down Regent's Park Canal. Tony was quiet and gentle and he held her hand as she climbed onto the boat. She would have liked him a great deal more if she didn't have Lawrence on her mind.

"Have you two known each other long?" she asked, as they seated themselves.

"We've been sharing the apartment for almost three years now. We get along pretty well. Lawrence is out most of the time, of course. Has a lot of girl friends. He's very attractive to women."

"Ye-es," said Carol, not particularly relishing this piece of information. "What about you?" she asked.

"Oh . . . I was engaged last year, for a while. It fell through."

"Oh, I'm sorry. I was engaged, too, and that fell through, as well. It's awful, isn't it?" She looked at him with genuine sympathy, seeing him for the first time. He had nice smiling blue eyes, but now she could see wariness creeping into them.

"Next time I'll be more careful," said Tony. "Not to rush into anything."

"Lawrence . . . isn't engaged?" she asked.

"Lawrence isn't the marrying kind," Tony said briefly. Then he looked at her seriously and said, "Look, this isn't my business, but you've been hurt once and I know what that means. I saw the way you were looking at Lawrence last night and . . . well, be careful."

"Lawrence," said Carol with some difficulty, "was looking at me, too."

"Yes," said Tony sadly. "He looks at all women like that, just as if they're the only one in the world. Carol, listen. You said you already have a boyfriend, so stick to him."

"But I—"

"It's a challenge to Lawrence, you see. I've seen him do it. He likes to take a girl away from her boyfriend, and when he's done that there's no more challenge. And he's afraid of getting trapped. So he drops her."

Carol's cheeks burned bright pink. "I don't believe you. I don't know why you're saying such things. I'm sure he's not like that."

"We both know," said Tony, "that some people are just like that."

"But not Lawrence. I'm sure he's not. You shouldn't talk like that about someone who's been your friend for three years. I think . . . why, you must be jealous!"

Tony looked away from her at the passing canal banks. "I was afraid you'd take it like that. All right, it's none of my business. I like you, I don't want to see you hurt, that's all. Not that Lawrence means to hurt people. It's compulsive; he can't help it."

"Thanks, but I won't get hurt," said Carol, and tilting her chin in the air, she turned her head to look at the other side of the canal. She was extremely aloof with Tony after that.

"What d'you think of that?" she asked, once he'd taken her home and left. "It wasn't true, was it?"

"How would I know?" said James.

"I thought Tony was nice," she said.

"Perhaps he is," said James.

At which point the phone rang and it was Lawrence. He had spent the day at his mother's, he said, and had just arrived home. Would Carol like to have a drink with him?

They sipped cocktails at a hotel with a very pretty garden. Lawrence held Carol's hand and told her about his mother, whom he said she must meet sometime. On Monday he took her to the movies and put his arm around her, and during the intermission he told her she was the prettiest girl he'd met for a long time. On Tuesday he had to work late. On Wednesday he took her out to dinner, just the two of them, and gazed into her eyes. On Saturday, after their classes, they made a beeline for each other in the cafeteria and went out afterward. This time Tony did not join them.

Carol was very happy. At least, she would have been happy but for James. Sometimes when Lawrence asked her out she found herself saying that she was seeing James that evening. "Just to keep him on his toes," James explained afterward. Sometimes, at moments that would otherwise have been rare and beautiful, James chipped into her thoughts with remarks like, "I'd take that with a pinch of salt if I were you."

When Lawrence said, "You have the most beautiful eyes, Carol," James burst in on her thoughts with, "Of course. He can see himself reflected in them." And once, when Lawrence had just taken her face in his hands and was about to kiss her, James said hollowly, "Remember Tom Everton."

"I don't want to discuss Tom Everton!" Carol said aloud.

"Darling, what are you talking about? What's wrong?" Lawrence asked.

Carol was dumbfounded. "Oh, gosh, I'm sorry. I was . . . I was sort of daydreaming."

Lawrence was not flattered. He hadn't so far actually said that he loved her, but it was quite clear that he did, as Carol kept explaining to James. No one could be so attentive, so interested, so loving, without meaning it. Tony had been wrong. Or even if there was something in what he had said, it was simply that until now Lawrence had not met the right girl, the one he would want to stick with. She, Carol, was the right girl.

Her mind became so full of Lawrence that James seldom managed to get a word in, but when he did his remarks were as cryptic as ever.

Sometimes Lawrence would say, "How's James?" and Carol would make some airy comment. The last time Lawrence asked about James was when they were dining at a little restaurant they had been frequenting. Carol smiled openly and said, "Oh, he's gone abroad. For his firm. So I won't be seeing him again for a long time. If at all." She continued to smile at him, waiting for his response.

Over his face there passed a flicker of . . . could it be annoyance? "Oh, I thought you two had something going together . . . I mean, you've been seeing quite a lot of each other."

"Not so much since I've known you," said Carol meltingly.

Lawrence began to crumble a roll. "I hope . . . I hope I didn't break anything up."

"Oh, no you mustn't worry. We were just friends, you know." She leaned forward and laid her hand on his.

"I mean," said Lawrence, "I wouldn't want you to get the wrong impression about me." And he removed his hand from under hers.

"What do you mean?"

"Well, you're wonderful, and I've really enjoyed seeing you the past few weeks, but I'd hate for you to get serious about me." He smiled his enchanting smile. "But you haven't, of course, have you?"

Carol felt the pain in her stomach that comes from being punched, hard. James whispered, "You told Tony you weren't going to get hurt, remember?" Right, she wouldn't.

"Serious about you?" she said, smiling still. "I wasn't serious about James—why should I be serious about you? James is a very attractive man, you know. He asked me to marry him before he left, but I don't want to be tied down just yet."

"Oh, good. I mean, it's good you're not unhappy about his going."

Somehow the rest of the evening passed, and when Lawrence delivered her to her front door she was not really surprised to hear him say, "I'm afraid I'm going to be rather busy for the next few weeks. I'll get in touch with you in a while. Okay?"

"If I'm still around," said Carol, giving him a casual peck on the cheek and closing the door firmly.

She slammed her bedroom door, flung off her coat in one direction and her shoes in another and found a cushion that she proceeded to pound with furious clenched fists for several minutes.

"No tears?" asked James.

She sat breathlessly on the shapeless cushion. "No tears," she said firmly. "You were right and Tony was right and I was wrong. I'm angry, I'm furious, but—"

"You weren't really in love with him," said James.

"No, I suppose I wasn't. I did want to be in love with someone, though. And he is very handsome."

"Looks aren't everything, you know," said James.

When she went to the cafeteria after her class the following Saturday, she noticed that Tony and Lawrence were sitting at separate tables. She went to the corner where Tony sat immersed in a book on Spanish grammar.

He looked up, surprise and pleasure spreading over his face. "Carol! How nice. What, er...?"

"You were right and I was wrong," said Carol shortly. "I owe you an apology."

Tony flushed. "That's quite an admission. But I'm sorry. Do you feel awful?"

"I feel fine. It was all too good to be true, really. I think I knew that inside; part of me did, anyway." What would he think if she told him that that part of her was called James? Somehow, she felt Tony might understand.

"And why aren't you sitting with Lawrence?" she asked.

Tony looked over to the table where Lawrence was sitting talking to a blond girl. "You've got ink on your fingers," they heard him say. "Such pretty fingers, too."

"Lawrence can get tiresome after a while," said Tony meditatively. "A bit repetitive, if you know what I mean. I thought it was time I moved out. I have a place of my own now. Maybe you'd like to come and see it? I could do with some feminine advice—especially from an artist."

"Oh... artist! I'm just a Saturday-afternoon painter."

"How would you like to be a Sunday-all-day painter? The whole place needs decorating. It's a bit of a nerve to ask, but...."

"I think," said Carol, "that would be fun."

Several weeks later she was sitting in Tony's newly decorated living room. A painting of Regent's Park Canal signed C.V. hung bravely over the mantelpiece and she was cutting the last piece of wool for the cushion cover she had been crocheting.

Tony brought in the coffee. He stopped and looked around, then breathed a sigh of satisfaction. "It's all very domestic, isn't it?" he remarked.

"Yes. Rather cozy, I was thinking."

"Yes. Carol, I always said I wouldn't rush into anything."

There was a long pause. Tony set the coffee cups down and sat on the sofa next to Carol. He said, "That friend of yours—James. Whatever happened to him?"

Carol was surprised. "Oh . . . James!" she said. "He's gone away."

And this time, he really had.

PATRICIA CONDON

Let me Count the Ways

It had been a long, hard day at the library; a typical beginning-of-term day, with a continuous flow of new students clutching their lists of required reading and wandering between the shelves in search of Gibbon, Macaulay, Chaucer and Dostoevski. Since all the books were carefully categorized and alphabetically arranged, I never ceased to be surprised by the difficulty experienced by so many of these presumably literate young people in locating desired volumes.

"Either they're terribly nervous or terribly nearsighted," I told my roommate, wearily kicking off my shoes, "but I've been up and down those ladders so often today I feel like a window cleaner!"

"There's nothing wrong with their nerves," said Pam, closing one eye and applying mascara to the other, "or their vision. They just like looking at your legs."

"Pamela!"

"Well, why wouldn't they? You have very nice legs." Catching sight of my reflection in her mirror, she groaned. "Honestly, Liz—sometimes I think you were born into the wrong century. You belong to the Victorian era, when ladies were swaddled in bonnets and bustles and high-buttoned boots, with fluttering fans to hide their maidenly blushes. And, of course, blissfully ignorant of the facts of life."

"Hey!" I stopped massaging my toes and looked up indignantly. "I know the facts of life!"

"Okay. Let's just say you prefer to ignore them. It's true, Liz. Look how you reacted just now. Instead of being gratified that you're blessed with a pair of pins guaranteed to put a sparkle in the eye of the average male undergraduate, you turn pink as a prawn and bury your head like the proverbial ostrich."

"Well, make up your mind," I said tolerantly. "Which am I—fish or fowl?"

"Oh, very droll. Brian's right," said Pam, returning to her mirror. "He says you have a very sharp wit."

"Does he? How nice of him." Honesty precluded my returning the compliment, Brian's own conversation being so totally mundane that I failed to see how anyone as bright as Pam could even contemplate marrying him. He was, admittedly, extremely handsome, his perfect profile and fair hair reminiscent of the poet, Rupert Brooke; but there, I feared, the resemblance ended. Brian's deepest emotions could be stirred only, I was sure, by the fluctuations of the stock market. If I ever married (a contingency that, at the age of twenty-seven, seemed increasingly improbable), I wouldn't want a spouse who talked about unit trusts over the breakfast toast. No fear! "I want poetry with *my* porridge," I said firmly. Mind you, I didn't know I'd spoken aloud until Pam gave me a solicitous pat on the head and suggested I have an early night.

"I won't be home late myself," she said. "We're only dining with Brian's boss, and I suspect the evening will be one long yawn. Still, it's another hurdle in the promotion stakes, and if all goes well we could be calling the banns by Easter. I'd risk it regardless, but—well, we must be one hundred percent secure financewise, Brian says."

"Mmm." Hastily I changed a grimace into a grin. "Good luck—and try to suppress the yawns."

As soon as she had left, however, I found it quite impossible to suppress my own, and decided to take her advice about an early night, which was how I came to be wearing my nightie and dressing gown and holding a mug of steaming cocoa when the doorbell rang.

She's done it again, I thought resignedly, turning down the television volume. *And tonight of all nights! Brian will not be pleased.*

"Don't tell me," I said as I opened the door, my eyes closed in exaggerated exasperation. "You've left your keys in your other handbag."

"No," said a pleasant, courteous, slightly surprised and unmistakably masculine voice. "I haven't."

My eyes flew open, and my right hand gave an involuntary upward jerk, whereupon the contents of my cocoa mug surged forward like a small tidal wave, instantly transforming the front of the young man's pullover from pale blue to muddy brown. Together, in fascinated silence, we surveyed the phenomenon until, at last, I raised my reluctant gaze to his face, wondering bemusedly if he always looked like that or whether his striking pallor was attributable to the anguish of a scalded midriff.

"I'm so sorry!" I muttered hoarsely. "Terribly sorry! I thought you were Pam."

"No." Gingerly he took a fold of soggy sweater between his fingers and eased it away from what must have been an equally soggy shirt. "Browning," he said simply.

"Yes, well—" Helplessly I bit my lip. "If it's washed at once the stain should come out, but—"

"No," he said again, peering over the rims of his glasses. "I mean, Browning is my name. Robert Browning."

"Oh—really?" *Oh, really*, my whirling mind echoed despairingly. It certainly has been one of those days! "Look—drop it in a bowl of water and let it soak a bit," I burbled, leaning heavily on the door. "If that doesn't work, let me know and I'll gladly replace it."

"Thanks. I may also require a replacement for my right foot," he remarked constrainedly, "unless you stop jamming it against the wall. Please—I appreciate your skepticism, it's something I'm well used to, but my name actually is Robert Browning. You haven't noticed the new card beside the bell for apartment seven in the front porch?"

"No-o."

"I moved in a week ago. And we have passed each other on the stairs a few times."

"Have we? I don't remember."

"No, well—mine isn't a particularly memorable face. Also—" he removed his glasses and brandished them vaguely "—I'm not usually wearing these. I only need them for reading, but I forgot to take them off before I came out."

"Apartment seven," I said slowly. "That's the one just across the landing?"

"Yes. I've already tried the chap next door, but he's not in, so I thought perhaps you could help."

"Help? In what way?"

"Change." He waved a pound note and smiled hopefully through the intervening six-inch space between us. The smile and the absence of the glasses made him look very young and strangely vulnerable. "I haven't any change for the electricity meter."

"Oh! I see." Finally convinced and overwhelmed with relief that I was not, after all, dealing with a potentially dangerous eccentric, I flung caution to the winds and opened the door again. "I don't think I have either, but I'll check."

"Thanks so much." As he carefully eased off his carpet slipper and winced, I hesitated, assailed by a twinge of mingled guilt and concern.

"Does that really hurt?"

"It's nothing." He made a nonchalant gesture and nearly fell over. "Nothing a good orthopedic surgeon couldn't remedy, anyway."

"Oh, dear, I do apologize. First hurling cocoa at you and then crushing your foot—"

"Don't worry about it. Please." He had floppy black hair and one of his front teeth was very slightly chipped, giving an engagingly little-boy look to his smile.

"Yes, well—" My father's clerical collar would undoubtedly have spun around his neck like a hula hoop, but he was miles away at home in Nottingham, and this young man was clearly in considerable pain. Pain inflicted, moreover, by my own unreasonably excessive action. "You'd better come in," I said very quickly, before I had time to change my mind, "and sit down."

"That's awfully kind." He limped awkwardly into the sitting room and sank obediently into the nearest chair, looking around with undisguised interest. "This is very pleasant. Not fussy—but typically feminine."

"Thank you. That was our intention."

"Decor by Harris and Jackson, yes?" His smile broadened. "I noticed your names, you see. Which one are you, by the way?"

"Pam's Harris. I'm Jackson."

"Miss?"

"Of course."

"Why of course?" he asked lightly. "Don't you approve of marriage?"

"I most certainly do."

"Ah. Then your single status must surely be from choice, not from lack of opportunity."

"Mr. Browning—" I bestowed upon him the look that had never yet failed to quell the freshest of undergraduates "—I would suggest that you reserve the pretty patter for your contemporaries on the campus. You are, I take it, at the university?"

"Yes. But—"

"Reading—let's see—English literature?"

"That's my subject, yes. But—"

"First year?"

Under the full force of my Medusa-like scrutiny he continued, predictably, to wilt. "It's my first year here, yes. Miss Jackson, has anyone ever told you that you are astonishingly—"

"What?"

"Intuitive?"

"Frequently. And has anyone told you," I asked, momentarily diverted, "that you have an astonishingly large hole in your sock?"

"I know." Sheepishly he wiggled several pathetically denuded toes. "I was going to mend it while the Elgar concert was on television, only the electricity ran out, and—"

"Well, I'm afraid I haven't any change either, so—wait!" I said abruptly. "Elgar concert? What time?"

"Now." He pointed eloquently at the silent screen and there, sure enough, was a close-up of a celebrated conductor mounting the rostrum.

"Good heavens!" I leaped toward the volume-control knob.

"You, er, you like Elgar, too?"

"Like him? I—" When I was small, I had a spaniel puppy who used to sit at my feet and watch me open a pack of potato chips. He had large brown eyes, his name was Chips, and next to my parents he was dearer to me than anything in the world. Needless to say, he invariably wound up eating most of my potato chips. I looked into Mr. Browning's large, beseeching eyes and sighed. "All right. You can watch it here."

His face lighted up with incredulous delight. "What can I say?"

"Nothing," I retorted tersely. "In fact, if you utter a single word I shall probably ask you to leave. But as long as you are here," I went on, reaching for my workbox, you might as well let me darn that sock."

"Is there no limit," he asked humbly, "to your generosity?"

"Yes," I said succinctly. "The concert—and the sock. That, most decidedly, is the limit. You understand?"

"Absolutely." He nodded vigorously, arranged his lanky form in a position whereby his bare foot was modestly concealed, and fixed his unblinking gaze on the television screen. I began to mend his sock, the orchestra began to play—and for the next hour or so not a word was spoken. Frankly, with eyes as expressive as his, words were superfluous, his occasional glances toward me conveying quite clearly his appreciation of the music. Henceforth, I decided, I would think of him as Mr. Chips!

Then, sadly, it was all over, the last magnificent chords being succeeded by waves of thunderous applause and cheers to which I—and my companion—were moved to make our own spontaneous contribution. The resulting scene must, in retrospect, have come as something of a shock to Pam when, expecting to find me sound asleep, she quietly let herself into the apartment.

"Hello," I greeted her, switching off the set. "You're early."

"Yes." Pam's eyebrows were climbing, slowly but surely, toward her hairline. "If I'm interrupting—"

"No. The concert just finished. Fancy—if Mr. Chips hadn't run out of change, I'd have missed it."

"Mr. who?"

"Sorry!" Suddenly overcome with confusion, I threw the renovated sock at its owner, who fielded it deftly enough, but continued to stand motionless on one leg like a petrified stork. "Silly of me," I burbled blithely. "His name is Robert Browning."

"Oh, yes? Well, well." Pam swung accusingly toward my visitor. "What have you been giving her to drink?"

"But he hasn't," I interrupted swiftly. "Truly. *I* gave *him* some cocoa—accidentally. And then shut his foot in the door. And him in."

"She's raving," murmured Pam, holding her head. "Suppose *you* tell me what's happening Mr.—"

"Browning. No, please—" he lifted a defensive hand. "Don't *you* remember passing me on the stairs? Or seeing the new card by the bell for apartment seven?"

"Browning? Browning." Pam's face began slowly to clear. "Yes, that does sound familiar. But the fact remains that it's an unorthodox situation by any standards, but for Liz—well, I must say, Liz, I'm surprised at your entertaining a strange man in your nightie and dressing gown."

"Oh. Mr. Browning," I croaked feebly, covering my tingling cheeks, "you aren't going to believe this, but—but I'd forgotten that I wasn't dressed."

"Please." His eyes were now transmitting, with indisputable sincerity, complete reassurance. "I have three sisters at home in Cumbria."

"Cumbria," I murmured. "That's a very long way from here."

"Yes." He looked at me, and it was just like Chips and the potato chips all over again, except that Chips didn't have such long black eyelashes. "I must admit I've been rather homesick."

Behind his back, Pam was soulfully rolling her eyes and rendering a hearts-and-flowers mime on the violin, which I stubbornly ignored. "Now that term has started," I said, "you'll soon make new friends. But until you do, if ever you get unbearably lonely, you're welcome to come here and listen to some records or talk about books or whatever. Isn't he, Pam?"

My friend tossed her imaginary fiddle over her left shoulder and smiled bleakly.

Mr. Browning beamed. "You mean you're interested in books?"

"She'd better be," Pam said dryly. "She works in the university library."

"But that's marvelous! Miss Jackson—" he took my unsuspecting hand and held it fleetingly against his lips "—what can I say except—thank you for being so extraordinarily kind. Miss Harris." It was Pam's turn to have her hand kissed. "Good night, ladies. And thanks again."

"Wait," I faltered. "You still don't have any change for the meter."

"I doesn't matter now, bless you. I have a candle to light me to bed. Also," he added on a less poetic note, "an old bicycle lamp. Good night."

"Good night," we chorused.

"Good grief!" breathed Pam, closing the door. "Is he real?"

I sat down, cupping my face between my hands. "He is a rather . . . unusual young man, isn't he?"

"Unusual?" She was eyeing me thoughtfully. "I was going to ask how you, of all people, could have got into such a situation, but it's obvious now. That one could charm the birds from the trees—especially a romantic, old-fashioned bird like you."

"For heaven's sake, Pam, I'd ruined his sweater and practically squashed his foot. I had to ask him in."

"You were still taking a terrible chance."

"Nonsense. He was well-spoken, quiet and unassuming—"

"Sure. So was Dr. Crippen." She shook her head disbelievingly. "I still can't get used to the idea of your behaving so completely out of character. I mean, I'm broad-minded, but even I wouldn't dream of entertaining a strange man here on my own—let alone in a nightie!"

"Don't keep going on about my nightie, Pam. I've explained about that. I was very tired, and after the cocoa incident I was flustered. He had every reason to be annoyed, and instead he was extremely civil. Besides—" I frowned "—one can't seriously think of him as a man. He's scarcely more than a boy."

"Oh, yes? He looks pretty mature to me."

"I'm judging by his face, not his physique. Anyway, he's only a first-year student."

"Bringing out your latent maternal instincts, is he?"

"Don't be absurd." Making a dignified exit to my room, I said, "Incidentally, how was your evening?"

"Oh—boring, but useful, Brian said. You might just get to be my bridesmaid even sooner than we'd hoped."

"That's fine, Pam. Good night."

Always the blooming bridesmaid, I thought wistfully, climbing into bed. *Never the blushing bride.* Not that I envied Pam. Heavens, no. I'd rather stay single for the rest of my life than marry somebody as dull as Brian. It was only that there were odd times—and tonight, for some unknown reason, was one of them—when the thought occurred to me that it must really be rather nice to love and be loved.

"Guess what," Pam challenged as she came into my bedroom late one afternoon. "That was the florist again."

"Not again? Oh—" I put down my hairbrush and reached for the dark red roses. "Oh, Pam. Aren't they beautiful?"

"Beautiful. So were the ones he sent yesterday and the day before that. And the day before—Liz, you do realize that the only possible container now available is the umbrella stand?"

"Well, what can I do?" I looked up appealingly. "I've asked him to stop. I've told him it's becoming embarrassing, that he's being wildly extravagant and foolish—"

"Foolish—he must be downright bonkers. Either that or—" Pam stared back at me, her expression suddenly and mysteriously intent. "Liz, has he ever said anything to you?"

"What an extraordinary question! Of course he says things to me." I picked up one of the long-stemmed blooms and breathed in its sweet, heady fragrance. "In fact, we never seem to run out of conversation, that's what's so—" I peered over the rose at my friend. "What did you imagine we do? Sit and stare at each other in stony silence?"

"Liz," she said uncertainly, "are you being naive? Or evasive?"

"That's another odd question! Am I usually evasive?"

"No. But then you don't usually entertain young men in the apartment when I'm out. Nor go to concerts with them, nor dining and dancing. Nor do you literally let your hair down before bedtime."

"Oh—that." Self-consciously I brushed a stray lock away from my cheek. "Well, you always said the old style was too severe."

"But you never changed it—until this week. Does Robert prefer it this way?"

"I believe he did once make a passing reference—"

"Ha! I thought so. It all fits. The roses, the daily dates, the way he looks at you when he thinks neither of us is looking at him. Liz, he's in love with you."

"What?" With difficulty I lowered my voice to its normal register. "That's quite ridiculous. Why—he's a boy!"

"And you're a girl, my dear Liz. Which makes it a very suitable arrangement."

"But it isn't, Pam." To my chagrin I felt the treacherous prick of tears behind my eyes. "That's the trouble. It isn't suitable."

"Oh?" She sat down beside me and patted my back. "Sorry, love. I just thought, considering how often you've been seeing him and how happy you've seemed lately—I thought that possibly you cared about him, too."

"But I do!" I wailed, and buried my face in Robert's roses. "I care about him very much."

"You do? Then— Oh, look," Pam said vehemently, "I know I'm always kidding you about being old-fashioned, but you aren't telling me you'd let a trivial thing like an age difference come between you?"

"Eight or nine years isn't trivial, Pam."

"Are you sure he's that young?" She frowned dubiously. "He always strikes me as being far more mature than most first-year men. You don't imagine he's given a second thought to your age?"

"No. But it's high time he did," I said, mopping my brimming eyes. "I will tell him tonight that I don't intend to see him anymore. It won't be easy—"

"It'll be impossible. He lives right across the landing, remember?"

"I shall move. I was going to, anyway, after you're married."

"Oh, Liz." She regarded me pensively. "Are you sure you're doing the right thing?"

"I am. I never should have let myself get so involved in the first place. Perhaps if his eyes hadn't reminded me of Chips, it wouldn't have happened."

"Chips? Who on earth—" But before I had time to explain, the doorbell rang again and we gaped at each other in consternation. "That'll be him. Liz, you aren't going to cancel your date, are you?"

"No. Not when he's taken the trouble to book a table. I'll tell him after dinner."

"Mmm. Better do something about your eyes," she advised helpfully, "and powder your poor little red nose.

Meanwhile, I'll try to keep him amused somehow. I don't know anything about proper poetry, but do you think he'd like my limericks?"

"Oh, yes." I managed a wan but grateful smile. "That's one of the most endearing things about Robert. He does so love to laugh."

"I like Pam very much," he confided later, smiling at me across the candlelit table as the wine waiter departed. "You'll miss her terribly, I daresay, when she gets married?"

"Terribly. Robert—"

"Elizabeth?" (He had declared from the outset that he could never bring himself to debase so noble a name by abbreviating it to Liz; a sentiment with which, I could have told him, my father wholeheartedly concurred.)

"Look," I began waveringly, "I'm awful sorry. It's been lovely, but—well—it's got to stop."

"Ah. The flowers." He linked his fingers together and leaned his chin on them. "I know it seems ridiculous to have them sent, but I'd feel ridiculous carrying them along High Street. It is a fairly common masculine phobia, you know."

"I didn't mean the flowers. I meant—"

"Good evening, Miss Jackson."

I looked up reluctantly and recognized, with some dismay, a second-year student whose frequent visits to the college library had led gradually to our pleasantly casual acquaintanceship. "Hello, Malcolm," I muttered. He was a likable youth with charming manners, but I wished most heartily that he would go away. He continued, however, to hover, his earnest gaze now directed toward my companion. *That does it,* I thought gloomily. *Even Malcolm is only human. It'll be all over the campus by noon tomorrow. Stonewall Jackson finally surrenders to Babyface Browning!*

Robert, by this time, was returning Malcolm's smile. Of course! As both were reading English lit., they would know each other.

"Good evening, Mr. Browning," Malcolm was saying, and I was still wondering whether he was being formal or facetious when he added with enthusiasm, "That was a really great lecture this afternoon, sir. I was never very keen on any of the Lake Poets before—thought they were a bit wet, if you'll pardon the pun. But you've made me see them in a completely new light, and that's the general feeling of the whole class. Sorry to have interrupted, but I just thought you might like to know."

"Well, thank you," Robert said warmly. "I appreciate that very much." He watched Malcolm's retreating form before turning back to me. "Nice lad, that. Now—where were we?"

"Robert."

"Yes, Elizabeth?"

"Why," I asked him with utmost care, "did you tell me that you were a student?"

"But I didn't." He spread one large and steady hand over both my unsteady ones. "No, wait. That, if you recall, was an assumption you made the first night we met. I did try to enlighten you."

"I asked you if you were reading English literature, and you said quite definitely that—"

"That it was my subject. Which it is."

"Oh. Yes." I blinked. "Only not as a student."

"That's right. I did mean to tell you eventually, of course, but to be perfectly honest I forgot all about it. You never mentioned it again, and I had no idea it was a misunderstanding of any importance until tonight, when Pam pointed out, most tactfully, that you were slightly worried by the difference in our ages."

"Oh, no! She didn't! Robert, look—"

"I am looking, darling. It's incredible, but you are even lovelier than usual when you blush. And really, you know, you mustn't worry anymore. I don't in the least mind your being four years younger than I am."

"My fingers closed convulsively over his.

"But you aren't— How could you be that old and look so young?"

"I don't know. Good clean living?" he suggested piously, and began to laugh. "And I sincerely hope you aren't now going to tell me that you don't fancy the idea of marrying a doddering old don of thirty-one?"

"Marrying? Robert, are you proposing?"

"Trying to. Bear with me, won't you? It is my first attempt. I was wondering," he said, holding my hand against his cheek, "do you by any chance know Florence?"

"Florence who?" I asked dreamily.

"Florence, Italy, sweetheart. Where my illustrious namesake took *his* Elizabeth."

"Oh, yes. Elizabeth Barrett. How very odd," I murmured. "Only last night I was reading one of her sonnets."

"Which one? No—don't tell me," Robert said quietly. "The first line is, 'How do I love thee?' "

I nodded and shyly continued the quotation, " 'Let me count the ways.' "

"Could we, do you think, count them together?" he asked. "In Florence? On our honeymoon?"

"Oh, Robert. Please, darling," I agreed with shameless, unmaidenly alacrity. "Let's do that."

CATHERINE SHAW

I'll Never Fall in Love Again

A gust of wintry wind scattered the leaves from the trees in the garden. From her window Jacqueline Anderson watched as they fell into a mournful huddle on the lawn. Then the rain began. Sighing, Jacqueline turned away from the window. Autumn was so depressing.

Once it hadn't been. Once she'd loved the sharpness in the air, and the warmth and coziness indoors as the house took on its winter character with the shortening days and colder nights.

She'd loved even the leaves then, and had often gone walking with her daughter, Debbie, crunching across the red, brown and gold carpets in the park. But that was a long time ago when John had been there to share the laughter and the fun.

Bleakly she sat down and plunged the needle through the tapestry she was making, but she couldn't concentrate. Debbie clattered down the stairs and burst into the room.

"Mommy, what can I do now?" Debbie was small boned and fair like Jacqueline. But she had her father's gray, intelligent eyes and his quick, impulsive movements. She was eight. She had been five when John was killed. She skipped across the room. "Mommy, what can I play at now?" she asked plaintively.

Jacqueline sighed. Keeping a bright, active child like Debbie amused on wet days was a perennial problem.

"Have you finished the jigsaw then?"

"Yes. It was easy."

"Well, Debbie, I really don't know. Have you read that new book Stephen brought you?"

"Yes." Debbie nodded. "Is he coming today?" she added hopefully.

"Of course, darling. He'll be here shortly, I expect."

"Staying for tea?"

Jacqueline smiled. "I should think so. He usually does, doesn't he?"

As she spoke, her thoughts turned to Stephen Jenkins who, as Debbie put it, was their "best friend." A ripple of uneasiness ran through her. A couple of times lately when Stephen had called she'd had the feeling there was something more he wanted to say, but couldn't. And when he left at the end of the day, she'd sensed something had been left unsaid.

She was sensitive enough to guess what it might be. A man didn't lavish attention on a person the way Stephen had on her for nearly a year unless he was serious. Jacqueline knew he was going to ask her to marry him. And she felt guilty about her tacit encouragement, for she knew she couldn't marry him. Yet because she had let things drift, she could hardly end the relationship until he brought things to a head himself.

She knew now she should never have let Stephen into their lives, never have let him take Debbie to the zoo and other places or let him take both of them out. She should never have let him do odd jobs around the house for her, all the practical things that John had done and that it had seemed natural to let Stephen do.

She was aware that she'd made use of him, that she was going to hurt him, and she hated herself for it because he deserved better than that. But it was too late to do anything about it now.

"Mommy?" Debbie's tone was impatient. "What can I do?"

Jacqueline thought for a moment. "I know," she said, "you're so good at tidying, why don't you do the drawers in mommy's dressing table? They're in a terrible state, all the cosmetics and jewelry mixed up." She paused, then added as an incentive, "You can have any odd earrings you find and a bottle of perfume."

Debbie did a little skip. "Oh, mommy, can I really?"

"Off you go." Jacqueline smiled. Debbie loved jewelry and would strut about in front of the long mirror like a queen, wearing dangling earrings and dabbing herself with perfume.

As Debbie scampered back upstairs, depression settled back on Jacqueline. Maybe she would cheer up when Stephen arrived, she thought. And really it was hard not to be cheered by Stephen.

He was big and cheerful and seemed to fill the cottage with his large frame. He smoked a pipe and there were always traces of tobacco aroma left the next day, but Jacqueline didn't mind; it was comforting somehow, as though he was still there.

Stephen ran a bookshop in the town five miles away and it had been there, looking for a particular book one day, that she'd got talking to him. He had ordered the book for her, and when it had come in, he'd brought it out to her personally. That day they'd chatted like old friends over a cup of tea, and gradually he had slipped into her life.

But it hadn't occurred to Jacqueline until recently that he might want to marry her. She'd seen him only as a good, kind friend.

He brought her new novels and biographies, and he always had a stream of hilarious gossip and stories to entertain her. When he was there, the house seemed to come alive, but that, she thought, was only because it was so quiet all week, especially now that Debbie was at school and she was alone with her tapestries and weaving.

She had become interested in spinning and weaving after Debbie was born and she had given up work. Then, afterward, when it had become necessary to bolster the small pension John had left her, she'd turned her hobby and her designer's training into quite a lucrative business. And Stephen had helped there, too.

He'd found new outlets for her work and kept an eye on the business side of it for her. He'd said that as he had to do his own account books for the shop, it was no trouble to do hers, as well. She'd been grateful not to be bothered by profit and loss and taxation, and hadn't considered the dangers of involvement.

Now, however, she realized she could no longer take advantage of his friendship.

Stephen came at five. Jacqueline heard the crunch of his car wheels on the gravel in the driveway. She ran to the door and pulled it open as he slowly came up the porch steps.

"Hello, Jackie," he said, smiling. "How're things?" He dropped a quick kiss on her cheek as usual and filled her arms with flowers, beautiful red and gold chrysanthemums.

"Stephen, you shouldn't," she admonished, "They—They're so expensive!"

"Flowers," he said fondly, "are never expensive for people who appreciate them."

She smiled. That was typically Stephen. He always managed to pay her compliments without making them sound false or overfamiliar.

"Where's my best girl friend?" he asked as he came into the hall.

"Here I am, Stephen!" Debbie bounded down the stairs, and squealing happily, was scooped up in his arms. "I'm clearing out mommy's dressing table." She rushed on, "It's in a simply awful mess!"

"Hey, you're not supposed to tell tales." Jacqueline laughed, her earlier gloom dispersing.

Stephen set Debbie down. "Well," he said, "you'd better get on with it or you won't be finished in time for tea."

"We have a surprise for you for tea," Debbie replied secretively. "It's your favorite!"

His eyes twinkled. "Debbie, how did you know I liked oysters?"

"It's not oysters, silly," Debbie said, giggling.

"Off you go now," Jacqueline put in.

Debbie ran back upstairs. Jacqueline and Stephen moved into the sitting room.

"I'll get a vase for the flowers," she said, leaving him for a few moments.

"Is your work all right?" he asked from the armchair as she came back and started to arrange the flowers.

"Yes, very well. I've nearly finished that big order for London."

"You're really doing quite well with the store there, aren't you?"

Jacqueline smiled. "I make a living."

Stephen glanced at her quickly, "You shouldn't have to," he said quietly.

She concentrated on arranging the flowers. "Why not? I enjoy working."

"I didn't mean that. Of course you should work if you enjoy it, but you shouldn't have the sole responsibility."

"I don't mind being the breadwinner," she interrupted quickly. "Isn't responsibility and independence supposed to be what we women want?"

"Is that all you want, Jackie?" He was looking at her keenly, and she knew then that he was going to ask her today. It saddened her to know that he probably would never come again. Debbie would miss him.

Really, she told herself, she ought to marry him for Debbie's sake. He was good and kind and Debbie adored him. And wouldn't she be less lonely and depressed if Stephen was there every night, always available when she had a problem or just wanted someone to talk to?"

Yes, there were a million reasons why it would be sensible for her to marry Stephen—but there was one very big obstacle. She did not love him.

She had loved John too deeply and completely ever to love anyone else like that.

"I've been thinking. . ." Stephen began, and she panicked.

"It must be time I put the kettle on," she broke in brightly. "I expect you're hungry. Debbie insisted on getting your favorite walnut cake today." Nervousness had made her speak without thinking, and she added guiltily, "But pretend it's a surprise. I wasn't supposed to tell!"

"So that's it!" He grinned. "You both spoil me."

"You spoil us," Jacqueline replied. Then because that seemed too much like an invitation for the conversation to return to its earlier thread, she rushed on, "Come on out to the kitchen while I get things ready."

He followed, watching every move as she busied herself. She talked brightly about her week. There wasn't a lot to tell, really, but she was able to turn one or two encounters with neighbors and tradespeople into anecdotes that amused him. She didn't want to leave any opportunity for what he might have been about to say, although she knew it was only postponing the inevitable.

Eventually there was a pause in the conversation that she was unable to fill and he said, "Jacqueline."

Just her name, but something in the way he said it brought a wave of apprehension.

"I'd better call Debbie," she put in quickly and turned away.

He stopped her before she reached the door. His arms held her tightly and his eyes looked deep into hers. She realized she was shaking slightly, her mouth dry.

"Jacqueline, just a minute. I—I want to talk to you."

"Mommy! Mommy!"

With relief she heard Debbie calling, and as Stephen's hands fell from her, she turned to face her daughter.

"Yes, darling, what is it?"

"Mommy, look what I found! Aren't they beautiful? You could wear them if they were mended. Do you have a needle and some thread so I can restring them for you?"

Shocked because she hadn't expected this, Jacqueline just stared at the open heart-shaped jeweller's box in her daughter's hands. Debbie shifted it so Stephen could see. "I love pearls, don't you?" she said. "You'll look beautiful in them, mommy."

"Yes," Stephen replied softly, "she will."

Jacqueline stood stock-still. Neither of them knew what this was doing to her. She had forgotten she had stuffed the box in the drawer one night when the phone rang. She usually kept the pearls on the top shelf of the wardrobe with her other mementos, only once in a while taking them down to look at them and weep.

Now she stared at the smooth round pearls and everything came flooding back—only it was worse because of the unexpectedness of it.

She'd been wearing the pearls the night of the accident. A policeman had recovered them from the wrecked car with their other belongings and given them back to her. There had been several missing.

John had given her the pearls for her birthday. And that evening they had been going out to dinner to celebrate and, of course, she had worn them.

Up until then she'd never been superstitious, but often now she thought how true it was what they said, that pearls were for sorrow, and all her sorrows lay in that small, heart-shaped box.

The only clear memory she had of the accident was of the thread snapping, the pearls scattering, just as the thread of her life had snapped and her dreams had scattered.

Now the pearls were a symbol of everything she'd lost. She could never bring herself to wear them again.

"Mommy, have you got a needle? I want to make a necklace for you," Debbie insisted.

"No!" she said, too sharply. "Put them back where you found them, Debbie."

"But, mommy." Debbie was crushed by her sharp tone.

"I said no, now do as you're told!" Jacqueline snapped.

Stephen was looking at her anxiously. He must wonder at her making such a fuss, she thought, so she said more reasonably, "They really need to be fixed by an expert, darling. Perhaps one day I'll take them. Now, hurry up, tea's ready."

That night she looked at the pearls in the drawer and left them there. They might as well stay there now, she thought wearily. Once again Stephen had gone away leaving everything unsaid. She sighed as she got into bed. "I couldn't love anyone else but John," she said out loud.

When Stephen came the next weekend, he took them out for a drive in the country. Later they found a lovely tearoom with low oak beams and a stream outside where they had tea. The proprietor thrilled Debbie by showing her the old millstones and how the mill wheel worked.

Although they were often alone together, when Debbie scampered ahead in search of wildflowers, Stephen said nothing, and Jacqueline wondered if he had realized somehow that she didn't want him to.

Perhaps he would just go out of their lives as quietly as he had come in. The thought saddened her, but she knew there was no alternative.

Back at the cottage, when Stephen went up to say goodnight to Debbie, there was a good deal of giggling and whispering and Jacqueline guessed they were discussing her birthday present. Her birthday was the following week and Debbie loved to make a big fuss of her. But apparently this year Stephen was to get whatever she had decided on as a present.

Jacqueline would have preferred Stephen not to know when her birthday was, because he was sure to bring her a present, too. He couldn't know what bitter memories the day had for her. With a strange feeling, she looked at the two conspirators as she entered Debbie's bedroom.

They looked so close, almost like father and daughter. Debbie, she realized, could give her love without feeling disloyal. And in that moment, Jacqueline almost wished she could, too.

The following Sunday morning, Debbie rushed into her bedroom and threw her arms around her neck.

"Happy birthday, mommy. I can't give you your present because Stephen's bringing it, so you'll have to wait till lunchtime. He's coming around then."

Jacqueline hugged her. "I'm sure it's worth waiting for."

After Debbie had run out, she got up feeling depressed. She went to the drawer to look at the pearls and then shut it again before she'd half opened it. She mustn't be morbid today, she told herself. Stephen was coming and she must hide her feelings until he had gone.

As soon as he arrived, Debbie ran to him.

"Was it ready? Was it ready?" she asked excitedly.

He nodded. "Yes, and here's the card. You'd better sign it."

The card was duly inscribed by Debbie and the ceremony of presentation carried out.

"Happy birthday, mommy," Debbie said solemnly, and Jacqueline smiled at Stephen. He was a dear, letting Debbie wrap him around her little finger. She took the small oblong parcel and kissed her daughter.

"Thank you, darling. Now, I wonder what it can be!" She turned it over, shook it, listened to it, felt it, went through all the traditional ritual before opening it while Debbie, beside herself with excitement, shrieked, "Open it! Go on, open it, mommy!"

"It won't bite, will it?"

Debbie giggled. "Of course not, silly."

Slowly, tantalizingly, Jacqueline tore off the fancy wrapping and looked at the box inside. *It's a fountain pen,* she was thinking, *just what I need, the darling.* Then she opened the lid ready to exclaim with delight and almost dropped the box as she stared, horrified, at Debbie's present.

The pearls! Her pearls . . . John's birthday gift to her. Only now they were beautifully and expertly restrung, the clasp cleaned and brilliant. Her pearls . . . mocking her from their bed of white satin.

"Stephen got them done professionally like you wanted,"

Debbie said proudly, "and it cost quite a lot. Actually I had to borrow fifty pence from him.

"Mommy, are they all right? Are they the way you wanted?" Debbie's voice tailed off in disappointment and tears welled up in her eyes as she realized that her marvelous gift had not given the pleasure she had hoped.

Jacqueline could do nothing. She felt bewildered, deeply hurt. For it seemed that a terrible outrage had occurred, a sacrilege had been committed.

A great wave of emotion broke over her and with one anguished and accusing look at Stephen she placed the pearls on the table and ran into the kitchen.

She heard Stephen say quietly, "Run out and play in the garden for a bit, Debbie. Mommy will be all right in a minute."

"She doesn't like them," Debbie cried. "She doesn't like my present!"

Jacqueline gripped the edge of the table to steady herself. And then Stephen was standing there looking at her with anguish in his eyes.

"What's wrong, Jackie?" he asked gently.

And suddenly she was crying on his shoulder, pouring out the whole story, all the heartache and bitterness and what the pearls had meant to her.

"I couldn't wear them," she said. "How could I? I never wanted them to be mended . . . but Debbie isn't old enough to understand."

"And she shouldn't have to," Stephen said with a harshness that shocked her. "You can't live in the past, Jackie. It just keeps tripping you up and you're the one who gets hurt."

"I'm sorry. I—I can't help it." She shook her head slowly and began to cry again. It was no good, he'd never understand. It had not happened to him.

But this time he didn't hold her soothingly. He gripped her arms and pushed her away, looking into her face directly.

"Jackie, you can't parcel your whole life up and put it away in a drawer like the pearls, to take out and weep over every so often. The pieces of your life can be rethreaded just like the pearls."

"No," she said, "it isn't that simple. My life was John, and John is dead."

"John is dead," Stephen replied, his voice soft now. "You have to accept that, Jackie. Your life isn't finished, it just has to be different. You have to face the fact that memories, however precious, are only memories and no substitute for reality." He smiled gently. "Jackie, all you need is an expert rethreader, too."

"What?" she asked faintly, but she knew very well what he meant.

"I may not be as expert as the pearl threader," he said, "but if you give me a chance . . . ." He tilted her chin with his hand. "I love you, Jackie. I love you very, very much."

The words echoed through her mind and she suddenly had the oddest feeling, like a smile starting somewhere deep down inside her long before it reached her lips. It wasn't what Stephen said, but how he had said it. It had the effect of shuttling her feelings all about like one of those puzzles Debbie had where the little silver balls had to fall into their right places.

"Oh, Stephen . . ." she whispered, her head against his chest.

"I don't mind if you don't love me," he said. "I honestly believe that will come in time."

She looked up at him. "I believe so, too," she replied softly. She was still uncertain of her feelings, but she knew now something had been slowly happening to her all this past year, but she had refused to admit it.

Stephen held her close for a long moment and then led her quietly back to the sitting room. She didn't flinch or recoil when he picked up the strand of pearls and gently clasped it around her neck. Then he dropped his hands to her shoulders, drew her close and kissed her, not a friendly peck on the cheek this time, but a truly loving kiss, and somewhere deep inside her she felt a faint stirring of response.

Debbie came in from the garden and stood in the doorway, tentative, puzzled and still hurt. "Mommy."

Jacqueline ran to her, kneeled down and hugged her tight. "Debbie, darling, thank you for a wonderful birthday present."

Debbie fingered the pearls doubtfully. "You do like them, after all?"

"I love them," Jacqueline said. "It was the most beautiful idea and the best birthday present I ever had."

Debbie's eyes lighted up and she smiled with satisfaction. "I thought it would be," she said happily.

AUDRIE MANLEY-TUCKER

Such a Romantic Affair

"The advertisement says: 'To let for two weeks due to unexpected cancellation.' There's a telephone number. I'll phone right away," Flavia said.

"Stop managing me," I said—amiably, because Flavia is one of the nicest people I know.

I spent the next ten minutes persuading a woman whose hips would never see forty again that a black one-piece swimsuit was much more glamorous than a leopard-patterned bikini.

For two years I had helped Flavia run her swimwear and knitwear shop; it was she who had told me that I should have known from the start that Rick was the butterfly type.

I met him and fell in love with him a year after I went to work for Flavia. I was twenty-two and should have known better! Three months ago Rick took me to dinner at a very expensive restaurant and blithely told me that his firm was sending him permanently to their Aberdeen office. A great shame, he had told me sadly, that he wouldn't get down to London very often, but once he was settled he would send me his address.

Butterflies don't settle—and they never send addresses. After the first misery, the loneliness and feeling of rejection, I discovered that I was living in a vacuum where everything was the same neutral shade and nothing was worth bothering about. I didn't want people; I didn't want anything—not even the holiday Flavia insisted I needed.

Flavia came back from the telephone.

"You've got a cottage on the edge of Dartmoor for two weeks. It'll be a change of scenery for you, if nothing else."

So here I was, heading westward on a shimmering September morning, with a pile of books, my oldest clothes and a box of groceries in the trunk of the car.

I reached Okehampton soon after midday, and picked up the cottage key from Mrs. Humphreys, the owner, who pointed out the way to get there.

"Oakleigh is not a proper village, just a few houses, a farm and a post office-cum-general store in Mrs. Pedler's front room. Turn down the lane beside the post office, and there are two cottages at the end, just beyond The Shoemaker's Arms. Your cottage is Little Thatch and Mr. Whittaker lives next door at Windways. He lives there on his own; you'll like him."

I didn't want a next-door neighbor, especially a male one. Still, I had no intention of being sociable beyond passing the time of day and commenting on the weather.

The village was cozy looking. Little Thatch, unlike its larger neighbor, was white walled and furry roofed. The gardens at the back and front of each cottage were divided by a thick green hedge that was a bit too low for my liking. A tall man could easily see over the top.

Beyond the gardens, a field sloped to a stream beside which a plump, cream-colored pony cropped lazily. Beyond the stream, the hazy, deep blue moors stretched away, wild and free, on the far horizon.

Upstairs in the Little Thatch was a room with a tiny window and a sloping ceiling. I looked at the big, comfortable bed that took up most of the space and thought how pleasant and peaceful it seemed.

The deep, velvety silence was broken suddenly by the sound of a rich baritone voice lustily singing the "Toreador Song" from *Carmen*. It was a very good rendering. I crossed to the window and looked out; the song came from the direction of Windways, but I couldn't see anyone.

I unpacked, cooked a meal, then watched the sun go down beyond the moors; when it was dark, the sky was as thick with stars as a daisied field, and the warm air smelled sweetly of honeysuckle. At intervals I heard the singing; the singer was giving a fervent rendering from *Tosca* when I went to bed.

I slept dreamlessly. Next morning I awoke late to another warm, cloudless day. I put on a pair of very old denim jeans, a faded sun top and knotted my hair up off my neck for coolness. I looked hard at myself in the bedroom mirror. I am only five feet two and have always hated my lack of inches; my hair is brown, my eyes are brown, my features put together into a very ordinary pattern. What on earth had Rick seen in me anyway, I wondered dismally.

Mrs. Humphreys had thoughtfully provided loungers for her summer people; when I took one out into the garden after breakfast, the pony had gone from the field and all Windways's doors and windows were closed.

I decided to have a plowman's lunch at the little inn, and as I was about to open the front gate, a dusty white car came bouncing down the lane. It stopped outside Windways; the driver was a well-built young man with thick dark hair and blue eyes beneath dark brows.

He smiled at me and said, "Is he at home? Or has he taken Bella out for a drive?"

"Bella?" I said, startled, thinking that he had a nice voice. Rich and velvety. Not a voice to trust. He was probably an easy charmer, like Rick.

He leaned his arm on the door of the car, his eyes mischievous.

"Don't tell me you haven't met Bella," he said.

I distrusted him even more.

"I haven't met anyone," I said coolly. "I only arrived yesterday."

He laughed. "And you haven't yet met Mr. Robert Whittaker? Oh, he *is* losing his grip! You should be out with him on a lovely day like this!"

"Should I indeed?" I said, with several degrees of frost in my voice. "My plans don't include holiday friendships. I came here for solitude."

Afterward I thought it sounded curt and ungracious, but the charm, the easy laughter, the self-possession of this man—it took me back to the days of Rick.

"Better watch out for Mr. Robert Whittaker, Miss Whoever-You-Are!" he told me with mock solemnity. "He's the local Don Juan. Every time I see him, he has a different girl with him. Last week it was a redhead; the week before that a blonde. They're not all holidaymakers from Little Thatch, either. The week before last it was Mary Taplin from Bramblecombe. Don't say I didn't warn you!"

"The warning isn't necessary," I assured him. I walked out through the gate, closed it carefully behind me and walked to The Shoemaker's. The occupant of the white car had evidently gone to inspect the outside of the house and assure himself that the owner was out.

I ate my lunch in the cool, dim, nearly deserted bar. Don Juan indeed! *I suppose I should be grateful for the warning,* I reflected. *At least I can keep right out of his way, now that I know. Who on earth is Bella? The pony, obviously. Does Mr. Robert Whittaker ride around the countryside on a cream pony, ogling all the girls he meets?* On reflection, it seemed highly unlikely, I decided. Still, I was just a bit curious. Anyone would have been.

I took a long walk over the moors and had tea at a tiny cottage under the shadow of a solemn, gray stone church. It was dusk when I returned, and a lamp burned with a bright orange glow in the window of the house next door. I heard the neigh of a pony and a rich, happy voice singing a saucy song that I didn't recognize; but still I didn't see anyone.

I met him the next day.

"Hi, Bella! Come on, we're going out this morning."

I waited. I heard a neighing, the sound of a one-sided conversation and noises at the front of Windways that I couldn't identify. Firmly, I squashed my curiosity and held my book in front of my face; but when I had stared at the same page for ten minutes, I could bear it no longer.

Cautiously I crept toward the hedge. By standing on tiptoe I could see over the top.

A pair of bright blue eyes gazed down into mine.

"Good morning!" said Baritone.

There is nothing more unnerving than being caught out in the act of spying on someone. . . .

His hair was thick and curly, his face was tanned, his smile certainly wasn't the leer of a Don Juan. "Lovely day!" he said.

"Beautiful," I agreed in a small voice.

"I was about to come over and ask if you'd care to come for a drive," he said. "My name is Robert Whittaker and you are Miss Joanna Selwyn. Judy Humphreys told me your name when she came to check the cottage yesterday morning. I like to know my neighbors, even though they're all short-term ones. She says you're from London. *There's* a place I enjoy seeing now and again. Only thing is, I have to board Bella at the farm when I go away, and she isn't too keen on that. Come and meet her."

Don Juan, I thought wrathfully, as I walked down to the front gate. This nice old gentleman, with the snow-white hair and well-trimmed mustache, blue eyes twinkling in friendship behind his spectacles as he puffed away on his pipe? He looked like a benevolent grandfather, and he was seventy if he was a day.

At the front gate I stood and stared at a cream pony harnessed between the shafts of a trim little buggy. "That's lovely," I said.

"I thought you'd be surprised." He was as pleased as a child. "I bought Bella when I retired because you only need a car if you're going somewhere in a hurry, and I'm through with hurrying. Besides, you can't talk to a car when you're driving it. I'm off to Combe Bradley to see my granddaughter, Jenny. Coming?"

"Mr. Whittaker," I said, "you had a visitor yesterday—a young man in a white car. He says you like to date all the girls. . . ."

"Oh, I do. I don't feel right without a young lady sitting up beside me. Anything wrong in that?"

"No. But he gave you quite a reputation."

"Ah! He would!" Mr. Whittaker smiled happily at me, clearly enjoying himself. "He's jealous, that's all. If he came in a white car, he's my grandson, William, Jenny's twin. He has a very perverse sense of humor, Miss Selwyn."

Going to Combe Bradley meant getting involved—and I wanted solitude, didn't I? I wasn't all that sure, as I ran indoors to grab my sunglasses and my old duffel bag.

With great dignity Mr. Whittaker helped me into the buggy. Bella turned her head with a disapproving air as though she didn't like my outfit.

Mr. Whittaker picked up the reins. We negotiated the lane and drove past Mrs. Pedler, standing at the doorway of her shop. She smiled encouragingly at me, as though she had seen it all before.

"My friends call me Jo," I told Mr. Whittaker.

"I shall call you Joanna. It goes much better with this kind of conveyance," he told me gravely.

We went along a quiet back road, under a green umbrella of trees, past high hedges and sun-dappled fields. I drew a deep breath of sheer pleasure and said to Mr. Whittaker, "You can sing if you like."

"Ah. Did I disturb you?"

"No, I enjoyed it," I assured him.

"I only sing when I'm alone," he told me, rather wistfully. "My wife has been dead for six years. Twice a week Alice Hoskins comes up to see what I've been doing to the place. She might as well move in, I tell her, but she won't hear of it. When I was in business, I baked the best bread in the world, as well as pies and buns—and I iced all the cakes. I taught Jenny how to cook, and she's added a tearoom since she took over Whittaker's Bakery, Combe Bradley."

I listened, fascinated. Flavia would have called him a character, and she would have been astonished if she could have seen me.

"What does William do for a living?" I asked.

"William is the local veterinarian. A very good one. Dedicated."

Rounding a bend several minutes later we came upon a dusty white car parked outside a farm, and Bella automatically halted. Toward the gate came a young man carrying a case.

He looked at me and his eyebrows rose. I stared back gravely.

"Morning, William!" said his grandfather heartily. "What's all this Don Juan business, eh? Libel!"

William shook his head sorrowfully at me. "You didn't heed my warning. Weren't you the girl who craved only solitude?"

"I changed my mind," I said hastily.

His smile was wide and wicked. "It didn't take you long, did it? Was it grandfather's irresistible charm or the novelty of riding in a buggy?"

"William! Miss Joanna Selwyn is my guest."

I bent forward and smiled down sweetly at William. The idea of teasing this brash, overconfident young man was too good to resist. "Actually, your grandfather and I are eloping," I told him without batting an eyelid.

William looked me over from head to toe, then he roared with laughter. "Eloping? Dressed like that? How unromantic!"

He gave us both a "good morning" and walked, whistling, to his car. I recognized the tune: "The Lass with the Delicate Air."

My cheeks were hot. I felt plain and scruffy and furious. Mr. Whittaker patted my arm consolingly.

"Don't mind William," he soothed. "He's very young yet. Twenty-six. He doesn't know how to treat a young lady."

"Has he ever had one?" I asked scathingly.

"Several," said Mr. Whittaker.

We drove to Combe Bradley in silence. It was a fair-sized village, and as it was market day, Whittaker's Tearoom was doing brisk business. Jenny came out of the shop to greet us and feed Bella a bun. She was exactly like William in coloring and features, but her smile was kind and friendly.

Mr. Whittaker went off to do some shopping. Jenny whisked me into the shop to feed me cake and coffee.

"Grandfather brings all his girl friends here," she told me. "Don't look like that! Everybody loves him. He gave me the business and taught me how to run it. My parents are the itchy-feet type and they have jobs that take them all over the world, but I love it here. Go and take a look at the market. You'll like it."

So I threaded my way between crowded stalls under striped awnings and thought that Rick would have called it corny.

I bought a couple of secondhand books, homemade toffee, honey and some bits of old china I didn't need. Then I had to buy a rush basket to hold it all. I couldn't remember when I had last enjoyed myself so much. The day wasn't as neutral colored as all the others had been for so long—it was a lovely shade of pink, like the dress swinging from a hanger by a stall.

It was very pretty, a crisp print, with a low neck and elbow-length sleeves ending in a frill. There was a frill around the hem, too, and the pattern was one of tiny rosebuds. It wasn't me at all. My clothes are always matter-of-fact.

William's look had condemned my holiday gear as scruffy. Of course it wasn't . . . was it?

"It suits you, dear," said the woman who owned the stall. "All the fashion in London, you know."

I fingered the dress. It wasn't expensive.

"All right," I said, weak willed.

"What about the hat, too?" she suggested, her voice persuasive.

It was a clever idea. The hat had a pink ribbon around it.

"I'll take that, too," I said recklessly.

"So you should," said a voice I recognized. "It's a lot better than the outfit you're wearing."

"It's nothing at all to do with you," I told William in a subzero voice.

"Oh, but it is," he assured me with great seriousness. "After all, it's my grandfather you're eloping with, isn't it?"

The stall holder was goggle-eyed. An arm-in-arm couple looked at us with interest. I glared at William furiously.

He glanced at his watch. "I have to go; I'm due at the cattle inspector's office. I hope you'll both be very happy."

I grabbed the parcel, paid for it and scuttled back to the shop. When I told Jenny what had happened, she laughed until she cried; then she looked at me and asked, "Who took your sense of humor away from you, Joanna?"

"No one," I said slowly. But I thought about her words, sitting beside Mr. Whittaker as we jogged back to Oakleigh.

"Did you enjoy yourself?" William's grandfather asked as he helped me down from the buggy.

I planted a kiss on his tanned cheek. "Yes, thank you," I said. "I had a lovely day."

He looked wistful. "I wish Alice Hoskins was here now."

"Why?" I asked.

"It might have made her jealous—seeing you kiss me. I keep telling her I'm a good cook, sober, honest and thrifty. She says she knows all that, but it doesn't make any difference. She's been a widow for twenty years and likes her independence. Nothing makes her change her mind—not the blondes, not the redheads."

"Keep on trying," I told him. He was, I thought, a great deal nicer to know than his grandson.

When I drove into Okehampton the next morning, Mr. Whittaker was working in his garden and singing something from Gilbert and Sullivan about making the punishment fit the crime.

I bought a pair of expensive, fragile-looking sandals simply because they matched the ribbon on my new hat; and also bought several frivolous new tops and a swinging skirt.

When I got back to Little Thatch, William's car was outside the gate of the cottage next door.

I made myself walk slowly up the patch. I had no need to hurry, nothing to run away from. I hoped that I moved with dignity, but it's difficult when you're small and wearing flat-heeled sandals.

I was halfway up the path when William leaned over the hedge and handed me a box. He had a seraphic smile on his face. "For you," he said. "Grandfather baked it this morning."

Inside the box was a fruitcake. "That was kind of him."

"I can cook, too," William informed me. "It's a family talent."

"Yes?" I said. I smiled up at him. "It's usually the woman who baits the trap with food designed to prove the theory that the way to a man's heart is through his stomach. Still, I do appreciate the gift."

"All right!" said William crossly, as I went indoors. "So you got even for what I said yesterday. I'll tell you one thing—when I get married, I shall expect my wife to do all the cooking!"

"Haven't you ever heard of women's lib?" I called.

"Of course I have, and I find nothing in the state of holy matrimony that I like. Women are fickle, unpredictable, capricious, independent and exasperating."

At the door of the cottage, I turned. "Have you ever been crossed in love, William?"

"Yes. Often. Have you?" he demanded.

"Yes. Once," I retorted.

"That accounts for it!" he said triumphantly. "If you'd had as many bitter experiences as me, you wouldn't have taken it so much to heart."

I didn't slam the front door behind me; I closed it quietly and counted up to ten. I didn't *have* to see William again. It wouldn't be difficult to avoid him. I had never before met anyone who could make me produce prickles like a hedgehog.

I made a pot of tea and ate almost half of the cake, which tasted heavenly. When William's car drove away, I began to laugh and couldn't stop. I felt as though a great dust of wind had blown through a stuffy, airless room. I couldn't remember when I had laughed so much before.

I sat in the garden next day; the sun put a peachy glow on my skin, and I felt lazily contented. There was no sign of William and his grandfather had harnessed Bella and gone out early. The same thing happened again the following day. I was getting tired of so much solitude, so I went for a long walk, and when I got back Mr. Whittaker called to me across the hedge.

"Joanna!"

"The cake was beautiful," I said.

He smiled. "I'm going over to Combe Bradley again tomorrow. Jenny phoned and said I was to bring you, as well. Put on a pretty dress, there's a good girl. William says you look like a little boy going fishing in your usual outfit."

"Oh, does he?" I retorted. "Then that's what I'll wear."

"No," he coaxed. "I thought we'd take the Wrexton road to Combe Bradley; it's a pretty ride and goes past Alice's cottage. I'm sure you'd like to see her front garden."

I understood. "You're a wicked man," I said.

"I'm not!" he replied. "You told me to keep on trying."

"Where's William?" I asked casually.

"Out on his rounds. He got kept at Lewis's farm, Jenny said. He has a cottage the other side of Combe Bradley. We can go that way, if you like."

"No, thank you," I said firmly.

Weak willed, that's me. So I told myself the next morning, as I put on the print dress and delicate sandals and shady straw hat. However else could I have got myself so involved in other people's lives on a solitary holiday?

I thought about William, busy with pigs and calves, lambs and horses. It was probably a satisfying sort of life for a man, but didn't he ever feel lonely at the end of the day?

"Oh, you'll do!" said Mr. Whittaker happily when he saw me. "You'll do nicely!" *We might meet William somewhere along the road*, I thought, as I spread my rose-patterned skirt around me. *That would be nice.*

We didn't meet William. I had a silly, letdown feeling.

We stopped outside Alice's cottage while Mr. Whittaker loudly admired the flowers that lay, like a rug, over the stone wall.

Alice came to the door. She was a small, plump woman with curly gray hair. When she smiled she was very pretty.

"This is Joanna Selwyn," Mr. Whittaker said. "She's going to ride in the carnival procession with me next week; that old pink shawl you have would just go with her outfit, Alice."

"A treat," she agreed gravely. "Perfect match. You're welcome, Miss Selwyn." She came down to the gate, shading her eyes from the sun. "Come in and have coffee."

"We can't stay," said Mr. Whittaker. "We have to be at Combe Bradley in half an hour. We'll be back next week for the shawl."

He shook the reins, and Bella went off at a smart trot.

"What carnival?" I asked him suspiciously.

"The annual one at Oakleigh. Decorated floats and bicycles and things; farm carts and anything else on wheels. You know the kind of thing. I always drive Bella in the procession, with colored ribbons on her harness and on the buggy. It looks rather attractive. Last year I asked Alice to come, but she wouldn't. She doesn't mind lending her shawl, though. I thought perhaps she would."

He looked so doleful that I squeezed his arm and told him not to give up so easily.

Jenny gave us lunch. She said that William was telling everyone I was really a bit too young for grandfather, and anyway, no one knew yet what kind of cook I was.

When William called on me the next morning and asked if I'd like to go on his rounds with him, I said yes in my formal voice and looked at the rain streaming down the windows. It was a day for a skirt and sweater—*oh, William, where were you yesterday when I wore a dress with rosebuds on it?*

William wasn't at ease, either. He didn't make jokes at my expense or even smile much. We both stared gloomily at the gray curtains of rain sweeping low over the moor and closing in the view. The wipers scythed two clear fields of vision on the windshield, but there was nothing to see. We called at several farms, where William squelched through the mud and I stared at the gray world.

We got out of the car once to look at the shops. My feet got wet, and my damp skirt clung to my legs. We drank tea and ate beans on toast in a little café. When I sneezed, William said firmly, "Come on. Home."

"I'm all right," I muttered.

We got into the car, and he headed for Oakleigh. He was silent until we reached the lane. Then he said, "Who'd want to be a vet's wife? Living in the country on days like this? Especially someone who has been used to the city."

"Some people transplant quite well," I pointed out to him. "Anyway, you said you didn't believe in the holy state of matrimony."

He didn't answer me. I sneezed again before we reached Little Thatch, and he told me to have a hot bath and go to bed early with a hot toddy. It was all very unromantic. I sat in the bath and wept.

The unrepentant sun appeared next day and flashed a brilliant smile at everything. I didn't have a cold. I sat in the garden and put my thoughts in order. William didn't believe in anything; and this time next week I would be getting ready to go back to London, which was a long way from Oakleigh. William and I would have been totally incompatible, anyway. Somehow, that fact wasn't much consolation.

The day dragged on heavy feet. Mr. Whittaker worked in his garden and went through his whole repertoire of operatic arias. In the evening someone called for him in a car, and he went out, calling goodbye and saying that if William called I was to say he wouldn't be back until late.

William just might call after evening surgery, I thought. And it seemed a shame that the rosebud dress should be utterly wasted. So I showered and changed, put on the dress and sandals and brushed out my hair. Then I went and sat in the little porch feeling unutterably foolish, for as the evening wore on it was obvious that William wasn't coming my way.

The sun had gone down when I went indoors. I heard Bella whinny. She was on her own, too, so I took an apple and some sugar and squeezed my way carefully through the gap in the hedge at the bottom of the garden.

Bella was down by the stream. I walked toward her, calling her name, the damp grasses brushing my bare legs.

When she came up to meet me, whickering softly, I put my arm around her plump neck and felt the tears sting my eyes.

Her soft, wet lips took the apple and the sugar daintily.

"He doesn't want to know," I told her. "It's all wasted, Bella. The evening, my dress, the way I feel."

Her ears pricked; she butted me gently as though to tell me not to be a fool.

"Bella," said a familiar voice from behind me, "is the most spoiled pony in the world. She's given herself airs ever since the local amateur dramatic society borrowed her to pull Cinderella's coach in their annual pantomime."

Slowly I turned. I hadn't heard his car bump up the lane, but there he was, standing a few yards away. I saw something else, too, that made my heart turn double somersaults: a tenderness in his eyes that I'd never seen before.

"You look beautiful," he said simply. "I wish I could paint you like that, with Bella. The dress looks very pretty, Joanna."

"It's the one I'm going to wear when I ride in the carnival procession with your grandfather," I told him.

He shook his head, as he came toward me. "Oh, no, you aren't, my girl," he said masterfully. "I've just come from Jenny's, and I've heard all about that bright idea. You're coming to the carnival with me, on foot, and Alice is riding with grandfather. I stopped off at the cottage and told her so."

"What did she say?" I asked, fascinated.

"She said it was a good idea and she'd decided that no one else was going to wear her shawl, anyway," he said. "It seems she's had second thoughts. I've had second thoughts, too—about such things as matrimony. I think it's an excellent idea. Don't you?"

"Oh, yes," I said, as his arms went firmly around me. "Shall we discuss your second thoughts, William?"

"Later," he said. "Much later."

It was a lovely setting for a first kiss; down by the stream, with the primrose afterglow filling the sky behind us, and Bella, tossing her head, annoyed that she wasn't getting any of our attention.

SUSAN CRAIG

Everything Comes to She Who Waits

As a child I wanted to be a singer. Any kind, operatic or pop, just so long as I could bring joy to the hearts of an enchanted audience. I would have given anything to achieve my ambition—my floppy doll, my pale gold, naturally wavy hair. In any case, Floppy Doll wasn't much fun to talk to, and I secretly preferred black hair that was long and straight enough to slide the comb through without it getting all tangled up.

It was a dark day, literally, when I knew for certain my cherished ambition would never be. The rain pressed against the classroom windows, tossed there from a black sky, as Miss Philips pounded the piano. We were rehearsing for the school concert. Alas, in the sweet harmony of voices, someone was singing off-key. No matter how Miss Philips strained, first this way and then that, she couldn't pinpoint the culprit.

In desperation the poor woman made us step up to the piano, one by one, and sing a few solo bars. I had only croaked four notes (I didn't know it was croaking; I thought I was singing as sweetly as a nightingale) when Miss Philips looked at me sadly and said, "Thank you, dear. I think, Margaret, we'll give you a very small *speaking* part in the concert. Would you like that?"

I nodded, although I felt too choked ever to speak again.

If I couldn't be a singer, I decided I'd be an artist. I would draw those mischievous little elves that skip across the pages of children's story books. My fairy people would be instantly recognizable because of the artistic daintiness of their limbs and the delicate sweetness of their features.

A huge sheet of paper was pinned to the classroom wall. It was to be a collective effort, and each child was allotted a square of his or her own. I was entrusted to draw and paint a family of rabbits. In my mind they bobbed and romped and jumped in the most delightful and amusing way. But on the paper they became two immobile circles with ears. The tails, those cute little bobtails of my imagination, completely defeated me. Oh, life can be cruel!

I took a course in business studies and went to work for an advertising firm. I stuck on the stamps, made the tea and passed the rest of the day filing and running errands. I plodded on, regardless, for a year or two and ended up in an office acting as girl Friday to a man called Andy, who was seven years my senior.

He put brilliant copy to other people's equally brilliant drawings. Once he said, in admiration of a particularly splendid illustration, "Don't you wish you could draw like that?"

I replied, "If one's heart's ambition was so easily achieved, I'd be too busy fulfilling all my singing engagements to have time to draw."

He had a bony, handsome face, apart from his slightly bent nose, and yet in a funny sort of way it was this imperfection that made him more vitally attractive, plus, of course, blue eyes that were completely wasted on a man. Those eyes, surrounded by unfairly long lashes, gave me a deep, compelling look, and then he trotted out a couple of clichés that I thought were beneath his intelligence. Something about one's heart's desire being achieved in sometimes unexpected ways and that other corny oldie about everything coming to those who wait.

I made a face at him and dodged the pretended cuff he aimed at my chin. I was half in love with him even then and became a bit savage every time some drooling female wanted to speak to him. I'd hand over the phone with a terse, "It's Caroline" or "Glenda" or "Annabel" or "Mabs."

I found out later that Mabs was his aunt, Miss Mabel Rushton, the one who'd brought him up because he'd been orphaned when he was a little tough guy of six or thereabouts. I didn't mind him loving her, because I soon got to love her myself. She wore atrocious hats and laced-up brogues, and although she had the bosom of an opera singer, she had a voice comparable to mine.

Once I let slip that my parents were on holiday and I was fending for myself. She immediately invited me to Sunday lunch.

I said, "I wasn't hinting."

And she said, "I know you weren't."

I don't think she meant to say the next bit. It was one of those things you only mean to think and go hot under the collar when you actually say it. Not that Aunt Mabs looked all that put out, more sorrowful. "I don't suppose it's your mother's fault exactly, but if you belonged to me I'd soon put a stop to any finicky eating habits. You'll be telling me next that you're on a diet."

"Well, yes, actually I am."

"Humph! I've never heard such a daft thing in all my life. You're too thin as it is. Isn't she, Andy?"

"She's all right," said Andy, without particular interest.

"Humph!" she barked again. "She's like one of those stick people that children draw."

Despite everything, and just about everything was piled on my plate (I couldn't see above the thick, pink-centered slices of roast beef, the Taj Mahal of potatoes and the twin pyramids of cauliflower and baby carrots), it was a good day.

I'd imagined that Aunt Mabs would live in a moderately nice house, but it turned out to be the last thing in elegance and comfort.

I gasped and said, "Which bank did you rob?" And she rolled about laughing, as if she hadn't heard it a dozen times before.

She explained, "That's why I want Andy to marry a nice girl. He's all I have and all I have will be his one day."

"Don't look at me," I said.

"I am looking at you," she said.

While it was gratifying to have her on my side, she'd misconstrued my meaning. "It's not me, it's Andy. He doesn't even know I'm a girl."

"Yes, dear. It's all that dieting. Have some more pudding."

You can't go on pining for a man who doesn't see you except as part of the office furniture. All I got from Andy was the occasional vague smile to acknowledge my presence and a huge inferiority complex. I *needed* to meet Damian. It was at a party. Someone spoke my name. I turned . . . and there he was. Tall and golden, like a Greek god who had stepped down from a legend to enter my life.

I found him physically exciting, but everyone knows that being attracted to a person because of their looks is only one tiny step up a many-runged ladder. If you're not on the same wavelength you never get past that first rung.

"Maggie," he repeated, and his voice caressed my name. "Our hostess said this would be to your taste." I accepted the tall glass; the ice clinked as our fingers touched for a second. "She didn't volunteer the information, you understand, I asked."

Not only was it highly flattering, but it had first-time status. Never before had a man who looked like a young Greek god been interested enough in me to find out my name and bring me my favorite drink.

Just after midnight he said, "It's time I took you home."

I didn't bristle because he hadn't said "May I?" I was too relieved that midnight had come and gone without breaking the spell.

He pulled the car into the curb. He leaned over me and I held my breath, but it was only to unlock the car door. I couldn't manage the seat belt; I kept pressing the little black button that should have activated the release system, but in my nervousness nothing happened.

"I specially asked for this type of seat belt to be fitted," he teased smoothly—oh, he was very smooth! "I always knew that one day I would meet a girl I'd want to trap."

It seemed primitive, somehow, to be sitting there, a prisoner until he chose to let me go. But I liked it! He kissed my forehead . . . mmm . . . then he kissed the gap between my eyebrows, then he kissed my nose. My mouth, my poor, eager mouth, was made to wait—for three interminably long weeks.

He had taken my phone number at home and at work, but he didn't phone. I was just beginning to think that he wasn't the answer to my deflated ego after all when, just as I'd stopped hoping, he phoned.

Now Andy never answers the phone—that is exclusively my job—but this time, as though sensing something different, he reached out his hand while I was still in the process of rising from my chair.

"It's for you," he said, and he couldn't have looked more surprised had the caller been a little green man from Mars. "Some character called Damian."

I lighted up, I know I did. And in my agitation, I seemed to be grappling with Andy for the phone, not just taking it from him.

Damian repeated his name, in case Andy hadn't told me.

"Yes," I said, and it came out sounding like a contented sigh.

"I half expected you to slam the phone down. But Maggie, I couldn't call before now. I've been out of town."

Didn't they have telephones out of town? I said, "I understand."

"Bless you. What time do you finish work?"

I thought I already had. Andy wouldn't get much sense out of me for the rest of the day. "Five-thirty," I said.

"I'll be waiting at the door for you. Goodbye until then, Maggie angel."

I put the phone down and glared at Andy. He could have made some tactful excuse to leave the office and let me converse in private. I resolved not to do it for him the next time one of his many girl friends phoned.

"Are you old enough to go out with boys?" he asked, and it was neither a leer nor a sneer.

"He's not a boy. He's a man."

For once, no joke came. "Be careful, Mags," he warned.

I didn't know whether to be pleased that he was poking his nose in or pleased because he cared enough to do so.

When I waltzed out of the office building, I didn't immediately see Damian. Someone who looked suspiciously like him was hiding behind a bouquet of pink roses.

"Oh! Have you ever seen anything more beautiful?" I gasped, as he dumped them into my arms.

"No, I can't say that I have."

I blushed as I realized he definitely wasn't looking at the roses!

I laid my first-ever gift from him—or were they a peace offering—on the backseat.

"What kind of a day have you had?" he asked.

"So-so. It's always a bit like a madhouse at that place."

"Ah!" he sympathized. "And what you crave above all else is peace? A quiet haven somewhere far away from people. Leave it to me, I know just the place."

That wasn't what I wanted at all. I wanted everybody to see us. I was bursting with pride at being with Damian, so naturally I didn't want to be hidden away in the lounge of a select restaurant, behind a huge potted plant to boot.

When Damian said, "Isn't this nice?" I agreed, because it was. And I could hardly voice my one objection—that I couldn't show him off.

After a thoroughly delicious high tea—I had smoked salmon and a very large luscious slice of Black Forest cake—Damian said very regretfully that he must drive me home. It was barely eight o'clock when we arrived at my doorstep and I felt cheated. But he explained very nicely about the business engagement he couldn't break. He kissed me sweetly on the lips, and I wondered if I would ever see him again.

I never knew when Damian would phone to ask me out. Our dates seemed to go from one extreme to the other. One week I saw him every single day, and not once did he have to dash off early to keep a business appointment. But then, as though his work had fallen into arrears and he had to catch up, I didn't see him for nineteen days.

Once we were having a quiet drink together when we had to leave hastily because a client walked in whom Damian should have been entertaining.

I knew something was wrong when he suddenly stopped speaking in midsentence. "That's torn it," he groaned.

The cause of his agitation—and he had gone quite pale—was a striking brunette. She possessed the long, damson-black hair I'd once had a fancy for, but the style was too youthful for her maturity. There was a hint of petulance around her mouth, a hardness around her eyes. You felt she'd found out the hard way that life isn't all sunshine and flowers. Yet she was beautiful.

"Who is she?" I asked.

"A client. If she spots us I'm done for."

"Why? You're entitled to some private life, surely?"

"That's what I thought. That's why I put her off rather than you."

I couldn't believe it. "You mean it was one of those occasions when you should have phoned me at the last moment to cancel our date—only this time you didn't?"

"That's about it, my sweet."

Damian had put me first. I was touched. "Is there a back door we can sneak out of?"

Things were horrible at work. I don't know what was the matter with Andy, but he snapped at me all the time. I couldn't do anything right. It got to such a pitch that I thought, *another week of this and in goes my notice*. It wasn't enough that he hauled me over the coals for slipshod work. (Fair enough, I did make some howling blunders, but I wondered how efficient he'd be if someone was waiting to catch him out all the time.) What really annoyed me was the way he picked on Damian. The limit came when he inquired snidely, "And how was your date with 'father' last night?"

I lashed out in reprisal, "You're jealous."

"If you think that you have an inflated idea of your worth."

"Not jealous because of me. Because of his looks and position." Which was silly when you considered that Andy held a good position himself and was even Damian's equal in looks, I suppose.

A man knows when a girl is losing interest in him. At first, when her step isn't quite so eager as she goes to meet him and her laugh not so ready when he makes a joke, it is a suspicion in his mind. But when she constantly has to ask him to repeat something he'd said, he knows.

Damian's pride gibed at a girl being the first to lose interest. He had to be the one to say finis. He did it with style.

There wasn't anything odd in his phoning to ask me out to lunch, but it was something of a novelty to be taken to the type of place where people looked around to see who they knew before picking up the menu. I know I'd wanted to be brought to just such a place and be noticed, but that was in the past. Now I missed the obscurity of our discreet corner table.

He must have read my thoughts. "Are you wondering why I didn't choose to take you to 'our' place?" he asked.

"Well—yes."

"I want that to stay bright in our minds as a place of only happy memories. Oh, Maggie, make it easy for me. . . ."

I could have made it very easy for him, but I held my tongue.

"At first you were just another girl to be taken for a ride."

"It's been a nice ride, anyway, Damian." It was shameful of me to be frivolous, when he was playing his big scene with regal dignity and lots of drama.

"Thank you," he said, looking pained. "I won't be seeing you after today. I have grown too fond of you to allow you to ruin your life for me. It would be shabby to go on from here. You see, I can't offer you marriage. I already have a wife."

"And children?"

"A boy and a girl."

I was late back from lunch. "Don't put the boot in, Andy. I've just had the elbow, and that's enough for one day."

My words, humorously meant, snatched the look of impatience from his face. He sat me down, held both my hands and said in brutal sympathy, "You're well out of it. Want to talk about it?"

"Damian's married." I was laughing; Andy thought I was having a fit of hysterics. He drew me into his arms and made clucking, soothing noises. My head against his shoulder was a better fit than Cinderella's slipper. "I've seen his wife, only I didn't know it was his wife at the time. He said she was a client. She had long black hair, and she must have been quite beautiful once."

His lips brushed my forehead. "How could he do this to you?"

"When I think back, I realize that all the signs were there that he was married."

He kissed my eyelids, the tip of my nose. Just before he kissed my mouth he said, "He can't get away with this. You might not have the muscle of brothers, but you've got me."

I never really wanted anything else. Well, I did once. I wanted to sing to an enchanted audience, and even that dream came true.

My audience is the sweetest little mite imaginable. She's

our baby daughter (Andy's and mine) and when I sing a lullaby to her, her little face lights up in enraptured bliss.
Later, when she's grown out of the lullaby stage, how do you think she'll like my drawings of rabbits?

PAT LACEY

The Tudor Take-Away

From the beginning, Uncle Hubert had known what he wanted to do with Great-Aunt Sophie's legacy. Quite a sizable legacy, apparently, running into several thousands.

"We'll open an antique shop," he'd told Aunt Madge, delighted at the thought of all the china and porcelain, Chippendale and Sheraton he would now be able to buy with a clear conscience.

But Aunt Madge had had other ideas. Only then did Uncle Hubert discover her lifelong ambition to open a tea-room.

"We'll do both!" he'd said grandly. And to everyone's astonishment, they had.

The Tudor Take-Away was in Dilmouth, one of those picturesque country towns with a broad main thoroughfare and a butter market, around which the traffic trundled in an orderly procession. On either side beamed Tudor houses stood amicably next to elegant Georgian, and bow windows opened cheek by jowl with latticed casements. The sort of town, in other words, that the inhabitants tend to take for granted but that tourists visit in their hundreds.

The café had its original bottle-glass windows and a massive, iron-studded door opening directly into a raftered living room that accommodated a dozen small tables comfortably, and still left plenty of room for Uncle Hubert's objets d'art. A few explanatory words at the bottom of Aunt Madge's menu of boiled eggs and brown bread and butter, scones and jam and delicious, home-baked sponge cake pointed out that customers could purchase—and take away with them—any pieces of furniture or ornaments in the tea-room or on the first floor.

The arrangement seemed to work like a dream; apart from the odd emergency when customers might actually wish to purchase the tables at which they'd been sitting or the china from which they'd been eating or drinking. Then, of course, it was up to Uncle Hubert to replace them as quickly as possible.

Hard-up nephews and nieces could always be sure of a pleasant and interesting holiday job at the Take-Away. Over the years I had become deft at clearing tables at the speed of light and washing up china before packing it in one of Uncle Hubert's special boxes. Although I now earned a living as a free-lance artist, specializing in the painting of animals, it was a precarious existence largely dependent upon personal recommendation, so it was vital to have some other source of income between commissions.

Actually I'd been very occupied during the autumn with the requirements of an elderly lady who owned a stud of Dartmoor ponies and lived, oddly enough, in the Home Counties. She'd asked me to stay in her charming old house while I painted an album of her ponies, and I'd welcomed the idea. But several weeks of her somewhat eccentric company and my very drafty attic bedroom had made me jump at Aunt Madge's suggestion that I come and spend Christmas with her and Uncle Hubert and help out with the Christmas rush.

On the day before Christmas Eve I settled into my usual bedroom with a distinct feeling of homecoming and looked around with my customary sense of curiosity. For in Uncle Hubert's house there was naturally a very rapid turnover of furnishings. One visit I might find myself sleeping in a Tudor four-poster, the next on a roll-away bed. But this time I was intrigued to discover it was to be a Victorian brass-knobbed bedstead, complete with a richly colored patchwork quilt. To match, were a rose-sprigged pitcher and basin on a marble washstand and, beside the bed, a brass oil lamp on a fragile table of lacquered ebony.

I hung my clothes in a massive mahogany wardrobe and arranged my few possessions around the room. Then I donned the long black dress and red-and-white striped maxi-apron that Aunt Madge considered suitable garb for a serving-wench-cum-seller-of-antiques and quickly went downstairs.

Aunt Madge was looking harassed. "Would you serve the girl at the table by the Christmas tree, Barbie? She seems to be in a hurry."

Was it that, I wondered, glancing at the auburn-haired beauty drumming her fingers impatiently on the tabletop, or sheer annoyance at being kept waiting, if only for a minute or two?

"Tea and buttered scones," she ordered crisply. "Plenty of strawberry jam and make sure the tea's really fresh."

She then picked up her plate in a dismissive fashion and turned it over to study the inscription. It was, I happened to know, Crown Derby. She bent to study it more closely. "This might do very nicely as a wedding present from my future mother-in-law."

"You're getting married?" I inquired politely, brushing away the pine needle that had dared to shed itself on the tablecloth.

"Boxing Day as a matter of fact," she said complacently.

"I hope you'll be very happy," I said automatically. I wished she would decide now if she wanted the tea service, then I could pack it while she was having her tea. As it was, I would probably have to wash and pack it at dangerous speed while she waited impatiently.

In any event, Aunt Madge washed it and Uncle Hubert packed it while I dashed out to the nearby bank for some emergency change.

When I got back, both the girl and the tea service had gone and business was even brisker. It was at least three hours before I managed to drag myself upstairs for a much needed break. It was only when I put out my hand for the magazine I'd left on my bedside table that I realized it had gone. The table, not the magazine; that had been placed, along with my traveling clock, hand cream and other nighttime impedimenta, on the graceful antique washstand.

Everything was there except the wallet containing the fee for my recent commission. One of my client's idiosyncrasies had been to insist on paying me in cash. Not that I'd minded. As long as I had the means to run the little car I needed for my work, with enough left over for a new winter coat and the price of a concert ticket or two, I hadn't minded what shape it took. But to lose the money would mean financial disaster.

I suppose I'd been silly to put the wallet in the drawer of the little table in the first place, but it had seemed safer, at the time, than in my handbag. I'd completely forgotten the risk, at Uncle Hubert's, of having the carpet sold from under your feet.

My tiredness a thing of the past, I rushed downstairs to check what had happened. As I might have guessed the table had been sold to my auburn-haired customer.

"She said her future father-in-law would give it to her for a wedding present," explained Uncle Hubert, quite distraught. "And it just fitted into the trunk of her car. My dear, I'm terribly sorry! It didn't occur to me to look in the drawer. I just cleared the top."

He thought for a moment, then brightened visibly. "Not to worry! She wrote her address on the back of her check."

Amanda Morgan was her name and she lived, it was no surprise to discover, in a very fashionable and expensive part of London.

"I'll drive up in the morning if you can spare me. It shouldn't take long."

Aunt Madge told me not to worry about rushing back. "Just as long as you're here to help me bake for the Christmas tea party."

With typical generosity, Aunt Madge always opened up the tearoom on Christmas afternoon to entertain those of her regular clients who lived alone and might otherwise spend the day in total isolation. After a magnificent tea, Uncle Hubert would dress up as Santa Claus and distribute little gifts and then, with Aunt Madge accompanying on the piano, lead the party in the singing of carols and Christmas hymns. Afterward there were games, mostly of the pencil-and-paper variety, and then a glass of punch before everyone was taken home, either on foot or in Uncle Hubert's enormous vintage car.

Preparing for the party on Christmas Eve was almost as enjoyable as the party itself. The kitchen would be rich with the scent of fruits and spices as the mounds of mince pies, cakes and sausage rolls grew steadily larger. "I wouldn't miss the 'great bake' for anything," I assured Aunt Madge.

As it happened, an overnight fall of snow had turned the roads into icy slush before I set out the next morning, and it took me a good three hours' drive to reach the smart mews apartment. I stood between sentinel bay trees and rang the bell on a bright scarlet door. And waited. Nothing happened. I rang again.

A sleek Siamese cat sidled across the cobbled yard, gave me an inscrutable Oriental glare and disappeared down a covered path. Refusing to face the possibility that there could be no one at home, I peered after him. There might be a side entrance I could try.

There wasn't. But there was a small ebony table with a lacquered top. I let out a shrill squeak of excitement and moved swiftly forward, my hand reaching for the brass-handled drawer. No need to bother anyone, now. I'd simply take what was mine and go.

"Can I help you?" inquired a deep, calm voice from behind me. I jumped like a startled deer. I couldn't have been more shattered if a hand had come out of the drawer and shaken my own.

I turned to face a dark, curly-haired young man in sweater and cords with an open book clutched in one hand. Repressing a quite unnecessary twinge of guilt, I heard myself stammer, "W-well, it's rather a long s-story. Miss Amanda—"

"In that case," he interrupted me, his gray eyes almost disappearing into a maze of tiny wrinkles as he smiled, "why don't you tell it to me inside? It's a chilly day and any story about Amanda is bound to be lengthy."

I turned back to the little table. "Could I just look in this drawer first? It's all part of my story."

"Of course!" He came and stood beside me while I pulled it open.

"Here it is!" I straightened up, clutching the wallet of precious bills. "My money!"

"*Your* money?"

"Yes, it's mine!" Anxiety made my voice sound unnaturally high-pitched so that, even to my ears, it sounded false.

"All part of the same story, I expect?" His voice was slow and very deliberate. Almost as if he were a policeman!

"You surely don't imagine that I'd take something that didn't belong to me?" I snapped.

"I wouldn't have thought so." He sounded surprisingly gentle.

"Well, then," I challenged, "I'll be on my way."

"Without telling me the story? And before Amanda gets back? That seems a pity.

So he did suspect me! I began to bristle indignantly until I remembered that the situation must seem, to say the least, unusual.

"All right," I agreed icily. "I'll come in just for a moment while I explain."

"Thank you."

The interior of the tiny apartment had clearly been designed to provide the perfect setting for Amanda's glowing beauty; white carpets, spindly gilt furniture and long, brightly colored curtains. The Siamese cat stretched its silky gray body over a cherry-red hearth rug.

"Won't you sit down?"

I perched on the edge of a chair and thought that the young man looked most incongruous against such a feminine background. A deep, leather armchair with tweedy cushions would have suited him far better than the fragile affair he was sitting on. I wasn't surprised when the long, lean fingers reached for a pipe lying on a glass coffee table, and was amused to notice how he stopped himself in the nick of time from knocking it out in a delicate porcelain ashtray. Extraordinary, I thought, how the most unlikely people chose each other as partners in matrimony. Although, of course, any red-blooded man would find Amanda Morgan attractive.

Instead of the ashtray, he used the rear end of a simpering sea nymph floating on a sea of Connemara marble, then caught my eye and gave a conspiratorial wink. Before I knew it, my own face had creased into a broad grin and I felt myself begin to relax.

"That's better. You looked as if you were expecting the third degree. It's not, you understand, that I don't consider you a completely trustworthy person but as I shall soon be one of the family, so to speak, I do feel a certain responsibility toward Amanda's possessions when she's not here."

Put like that, I could quite see his point. Especially as her possessions would presumably be his and vice versa, in a couple of days' time.

"But you still haven't told me the story," he reminded me.

So I told him about my free-lance painting and the cash payment for my last assignment, and about Aunt Madge and Uncle Hubert and the Tudor Take-Away.

"How about cows?" he asked.

I stared. "Antiques and toasted tea cakes," I explained patiently. "No livestock."

He threw back his head and roared with laughter—a jolly infectious sound that had me joining in. "I mean, do you paint cows?"

"Oh, I see! Well, I haven't actually been asked to yet."

"There's always a first time. I have a rather special herd of pedigree Jerseys I'd quite like committed to canvas. Would I get a reduction for mass reproduction, do you suppose? Not that any are the same, of course. There's Boadicea, she's the boss. And Buttercup—phenomenal milk yield, that one. And Botticelli—a very voluptuous lady. Bambi and Belinda . . . ." He paused for a breath.

"I'll send you a price list," I promised flippantly, while my mind raced with absorption of all this data. So he was a farmer. I'd been right about the leather and the tweed. For good measure, I now added a shepherd's crook, a couple of sheep dogs and an outsize pair of rubber boots. Not that I could see Amanda against that background. Strangely I found I didn't want to see Amanda against any background and especially not in the company of this wildly attractive young man.

"Will it be all right if I go now ?" I asked pointedly.

"Oh, I don't know about that." His face had become suddenly grave. "I really think we should wait for Amanda."

"To corroborate my story?" I asked, bristling once again.

"Shall we say, to apologize for the inconvenience she's caused you?"

"But it wasn't her fault." I almost wept with angry frustration. I was also feeling extremely hungry.

"Have a cup of coffee?" he tempted. "Or a glass of sherry?"

"I don't want a cup of coffee or—"

"Well, what *can* I get you?"

"Nothing. Thank you," I added tersely.

"Not at all." The conversation flow was at a very low ebb indeed.

I had a sudden thought—one I should have had right at the beginning of this ridiculous misunderstanding. "Why don't you telephone my Uncle Hubert? He'll vouch for me."

"I really don't think that's necessary," he said, "although I must admit I'd be fascinated to meet him sometime. Where is the café, exactly?"

But I wasn't really paying attention. I'd just realized that telephoning a close relative wasn't such a good idea. Family loyalty could make him corroborate the wildest story. And then I remembered my recent client; she who had given me the wad of notes in the first place. Mrs. Digby-Danvers was a lady of considerable reputation—and undoubted integrity—and being a person of somewhat eccentric habits, particularly where money was concerned, might easily have kept a record of the numbers on the bills. That would prove, beyond all possible doubt, my right to the wallet on the table between us.

The words tumbling over each other in my anxiety to be gone before Amanda should return and start wrapping this sizable young man around her little finger, I suggested this possible course of action to my watchdog.

He glanced at the gilt carriage-clock on the mantelpiece. "She's probably having her lunch at the moment. Like any sensible person. Why don't we do the same?"

"I couldn't possibly."

"Why ever not? I can grill a reasonable chop and I happen to know there's a couple sitting in Amanada's refrigerator."

Ignoring the hollowness of my insides, I shook my head firmly. But my stomach's sense of priorities was totally opposed to my brain's; it let out a rumble of most unladylike proportions. Before the echoes had had time to die away, the young man was on his feet.

"You just sit there while I go and fix the chops," he said tactfully. "There might even be a few tomatoes to go with them. And then if Amanda's not back by the time we've finished eating, I promise you I won't stand in your way if you still want to leave." Weakly I gave in.

Had the circumstances been different, nothing would

have given me greater pleasure than to have helped the young man to prepare our meal. But the thought of being confined in a kitchen with this tall, good-looking character made my pulse quicken alarmingly. I've always been attracted to outdoor men, especially if they have an indoor sort of mind.

Instinctively my hands sought refuge in doing something familiar. I took pad and pencil out of my handbag and started sketching the cat—still asleep on the rug. I had just managed to catch the fluid curve of his body from nose to tail, when the young man came back.

"Shall we eat here or in the kitchen? Hey! That's good."

He bent over me to study the little sketch more closely. His hand came out to lift it, and almost without thinking, I found myself turning my face into the comforting warmth of his arm. I glanced up to find him not studying the sketch at all but gazing intently down at me. I had the delicious feeling that any moment now both his arms would be around me and his lips closing over mine.

As if I were fighting my way up from the bottom of a deep pool, I suddenly shook my head and turned away. All that I really knew about this man was that he was going to marry Amanda Morgan and that he didn't trust me. The fact that I was beginning to distrust myself and my wayward feelings didn't help matters.

He, too, drew back, blinked and looked down at the sketch again. "Why don't I have this as a little extra wedding present for Amanda? You can finish it some other time. Just put your name and address on the back."

"Just like a check, you mean? In case it bounces?" I was on my feet now, glaring furiously, too confused to realize it was quite a reasonable suggestion if he really did want the sketch to be finished. All I could see was that it was his way of keeping tabs on me; of checking my integrity if Amanda wasn't back soon enough to prove it.

He looked at me and I knew that for the first time he, too, was really angry.

"If you feel like that, I wouldn't dream of keeping you a moment longer," he said icily.

Ten minutes later I was sitting in the car munching a sandwich and salting it with my foolish tears. And the wallet in my handbag was of no consolation at all. What was money compared with hurt pride and, I had to admit, a heart I could no longer call my own?

As I drove out of London, the Christmas trees sparkling bravely in all the shop windows did nothing to remove my misery. I felt about as festive as a frozen turkey. And I doubted my capacity to defrost in time for tomorrow.

In fact, by the time I reached home, the whole of my body was like an enormous icicle—except for my head. That was a furnace of throbbing pain.

Aunt Madge took one look at me and said, "Bed for you, child."

"What about the café?" I protested feebly.

"No problem! Mrs. Philpott's eldest is home from college and looking for some holiday work."

I argued no more. The thought of that warm bed was irresistible.

The rest of Christmas Eve was like a tunnel of feverish gloom, with Aunt Madge or Uncle Hubert—and once a dapper bespectacled little man with a black bag—appearing at the end of it from time to time. That I once thought Uncle Hubert had shed about thirty years and grown a thick crop of curly black hair was an indication of the severity of my delerium. But by Christmas day the fever had passed and I wanted only to sleep.

Perhaps, I thought hopefully as I drifted off, I might even manage to get up for the tea party.

I didn't, of course. I awoke to the sound of the first guests arriving and lay back thinking how ridiculous it was that I should still feel so weak.

Judging by the talk and laughter drifting up from below, they certainly weren't missing me. Large, fat tears of self-pity welled up and overflowed upon my cheeks. And once again there was a vast, unromantic void where my stomach should have been.

There came a gentle tap on the door. "Co-ome in!" I hiccuped. Santa Claus put his head around the door. I managed a feeble smile. And another hiccup.

"You're hungry!" he growled, in the gruff tone Uncle Hubert always considers befitting to his role.

Between hiccups, I nodded hopefully. He gave a thumbs-up sign then turned and went out of the room.

Seconds later he was back with a cup of tea and a plate of turkey sandwiches, which he placed carefully on the rickety bamboo affair that was now doing service as my bedside table.

"Eat up!" said Uncle Humbert as he sat down on the edge of the bed, presumably to make sure that I did. Not that I needed any persuasion. I was starting on my sixth sandwich when I noticed his hands. Long and lean, and, apart from the short but well-kept nails, utterly unlike Uncle Hubert's. And yet they were strangely familiar. As I peered, they were hurriedly withdrawn into the folds of the wide, scarlet sleeves.

"Who are you?" I quavered, suddenly conscious of my disheveled appearance.

"You shouldn't ask Santa Claus that. It saps his confidence, you know."

Now he was using his own voice. A voice that I recognized immediately. I put out an unsteady hand and pulled back the fur-trimmed hood. Amanda Morgan's fiancé smiled at me disarmingly. "Merry Christmas, Barbie!"

"Merry Chrristmas!" I quavered back. "How did you get here?"

"I wish I could say by reindeer. But actually my old Land Rover brought me, and it took the best part of yesterday afternoon and evening. When it comes to remembering exactly where she's been, Amanda's so vague it isn't funny. And you didn't exactly help—refusing to give me your name and address."

"I thought—"

"I know exactly what you thought and the less said about that the better."

He leaned across and took the crumbling fragments of the turkey sandwich from my unresisting fingers. Then imprisoned them in a grip that had my temperature soaring madly all over again.

"Where's Amanda now?" I croaked.

"Getting ready for tomorrow."

"Why aren't you with her?"

"Because I'd much rather be with you. And surely it's enough that I'm allowing her to marry my cousin tomorrow without sacrificing Christmas Day to her, as well."

"Your cousin?"

"Arthur by name. Mine's Ben, by the way."

I managed a grin. "Boadicea, Bambi, Belinda. . . ."

"And now, Ben! When Amanda told me she'd heard your aunt calling you Barbie, I knew I had to find you! But, seriously, did you know the doctor says you're not infectious any longer?"

It was the first time I'd been so properly and thoroughly kissed by Santa Claus. And somehow I didn't think it would be the last!

JANICE GRAY

A Donkey Called Delphinia

I stood by my hotel window that first evening in Crete, pleasantly aware of the hot, sweet, dusty smell of fig leaves mingling with the more aromatic scents of rosemary and wild thyme, and watching the sun sink far below the rim of Homer's "wine-dark sea." Somewhere in the distance I could hear the strange, haunting music of the bouzouki, and I sighed a little as I turned away to finish my unpacking.

If only Philip was here now enjoying this beautiful island with me, everything would be perfect. But he wasn't. I was here on my own, with not even a pale band at the base of the third finger of my left hand to show where once his ring had been.

Perhaps, however, I reflected as I arranged my creams and sunburn lotions on a glass-topped dressing table, that was just as well, since surely my primary object in coming to Greece was to show the world how little I really cared about my dead romance. Amazingly I had even managed to fool my mother.

"Crete?" she said blankly when I announced where I was going to spend my summer holiday. "Crete? On your own? But, Sally, darling—are you sure? I mean, that's where you and Philip were planning to spend your honeymoon."

She stopped abruptly, looking pink and confused, and I laughed and kissed her lightly.

"It's all right, mother. Really it is. I don't mind your mentioning Philip in the least. I'm over him now," I told her, fervently hoping that the recording angel would forgive me the white lie. And then, as mother looked relieved,

I added defiantly, "You know how much I've always wanted to visit Greece. There's no earthly reason why I shouldn't enjoy Crete on my own, now is there?"

"Well—no, I suppose not, as long as you choose a decent hotel," mother said doubtfully—so doubtfully that in the end it was to put her fears at rest that I'd booked a room in this vast, modern hotel, complete with sauna and swimming pool, instead of finding myself some small, family-run *taverna*, which is what I would infinitely have preferred. I didn't really like big hotels, but darling mother felt that it was the only way to be reasonably sure there was nothing too drastically wrong with either the drains or the water supply!

Now comfortably ensconced in the hotel restaurant, I ordered a cup of coffee to round off my meal.

"Have it with me," suggested a deep, lazy voice, and I was so surprised that I jumped, spun around in my chair and found myself staring into a pair of deep-set gray eyes.

"Simon!" I said incredulously.

Simon Rochford, the veterinary surgeon for whom I had worked until I'd moved to London in order to be closer to Philip, smiled. His lean brown face, attractive despite the somewhat irregular features, wore a sardonic expression that—even though I hadn't seen him for nearly a year—I remembered only too well.

He pulled out a chair and sat down. "Hello, Sally," he said coolly.

For a moment I was speechless, then with an effort I pulled myself together. "Simon, what on earth are *you* doing here?" I demanded.

"I'm on holiday, of course. I've been here for a few days already," Simon explained.

I sat back in my chair almost dazedly. Somehow, Simon was the last person I would ever have expected to meet in a Greek luxury hotel. He belonged—oh, he belonged to a completely different world, a world that I had given up, of muddy farmyards and sick animals and the stark beauty of the Cumbrian fells. Philip had once derisively called him earthy, and in my infatuation I had agreed. Earthy he was, compared with Philip, whose movie-star good looks and suave charm had swept me completely off my feet.

"Wh-what an extraordinary coincidence!" I managed to stutter.

"Isn't it?" There was a mocking gleam in Simon's eyes. Then he noticed my bare left hand holding my coffee cup, and almost without thinking I buried it hastily in my lap. His smile vanished.

"It's all right, Sally. You don't have to explain anything. I heard via the local grapevine that your engagement was off," he said quietly.

I stiffened. "Before you go any further let me tell you that I don't want any sympathy."

Simon's brows shot up. "Sympathy? What on earth makes you think that I meant to offer you sympathy? Congratulations is more like it!" he retorted.

I stared at him. "C-congratulations?"

"On getting rid of that stuffed shirt. You were always far too good for a pompous ass like Philip Marshall, Sally. I could never understand why a seemingly sensible girl like you fell for him in the first place. You should have looked at his lips," Simon said in a matter-of-fact way.

For a moment outrage struggled with curiosity. Curiosity won. "What have Philip's lips got to do with anything?" I asked.

"They're much too thin, denoting a lack of emotion or enthusiasm." Simon grinned at my expression. "Didn't you know that I was a student of physiognomy?"

Of course he was joking, but suddenly I found myself realizing how little, in fact, I really did know about Simon. I'd only been working for him for about six months before I'd met Philip, who'd been visiting an aunt in the Lake District and who'd gone to a great deal of trouble to persuade me that I would be far happier working as a private secretary in London than as an assistant to a country veterinarian.

Simon had never given me the slightest indication that he was sorry to see me go and that had hurt a little, because to begin with, at any rate, I'd liked him quite a lot. I'd been impressed by his skill as a vet, and I'd come to suspect that despite his somewhat taciturn manner he had a surprisingly kind heart.

It was only after Philip had arrived on the scene that he'd become hypercritical and in the end I'd reluctantly decided that Philip was perfectly right and that it really was high time I moved on to better things.

Now, somewhat defensively, I said, "If you didn't like Philip, why didn't you say so at the time?"

Simon shrugged. "My dear girl, it wasn't any of my business, was it? Besides, you were so besotted that I don't suppose it would have made the slightest difference." He hesitated. Then with a diffidence that was oddly touching, coming from him, he added, "I don't want to pry, but just as a matter of interest—what did go wrong between you and Philip? Who got cold feet?"

Somehow I didn't resent the question—not from Simon. "Philip. He met somebody else and decided that she was very much more suitable to be a senior executive's wife than I was."

Simon shook his head. "You had a lucky escape."

"I'd like to think so." I answered mechanically, but suddenly, to my enormous surprise, I found I really did think so. Perhaps it was because for the first time I realized that Philip *was* a little pompous, and he'd probably be even worse in a few years.

Simon glanced at me and then deliberately changed the subject. "So here we are, both in Crete. What are you doing tomorrow, Sally? I thought of going to Knossos, if you'd like to join me."

I hesitated, sorely tempted, then shook my head and said that I thought I'd rather explore on my own. It wasn't true, but I was afraid that Simon's invitation had been prompted either by politeness or kindheartedness, and I didn't want him to think that just because once—aeons ago—our paths had crossed, he now had to concern himself with my welfare.

I think perhaps I rather hoped he'd try to persuade me to change my mind, but he didn't, and the next day when I set out to explore Aghios Georgios, I was alone.

I didn't mind too much (except that I kept wondering why I hadn't seen Simon at breakfast) because there was so much I wanted to see. For an hour or so I wandered around the village that was basically just a jumble of dusty, shuttered houses and cobbled streets surrounding a small square where old men drowsed in the sun and small children played in the dust alongside a few hens and some very thin cats.

It was hot, the early September sun blazing through my thin cotton shirt, so eventually I made my way to the beach. As yet it was not too crowded, but after taking off my sandals and dabbling my toes in the water for a little while, I decided to do some more exploring.

This time I followed a narrow, meandering track that took me out of the village, past a small, snow-white church and tiny cottages with well-kept gardens, fragrant with herbs, to where there were open fields dotted here and there with whirling windmills that looked rather like giant rotating daisies. Butterflies floated like flower petals in the golden light, and there was a drowsy humming of insects, but I didn't see a soul until I met a small boy leading a donkey.

The child looked about nine or ten and was thin and dark with sun-browned skin and huge dark eyes that were nearly as soulful as the donkey's. It was a very pretty donkey. It had a rich, dark brown coat and little white socks over tiny polished hooves, and because I had a soft spot for all animals—that was why I had gone to work for Simon in the first place—I stopped to stroke its soft, velvety muzzle.

"Aren't you a nice little thing!" I said in English, and the child smiled.

"Her name is Delphinia and she is all mine," he said proudly. "My name is Niko."

I stared at him in astonishment. "Goodness! You speak English!" I said feebly, and Niko's grin became even wider.

"My brother, he teach me," he explained. "He is waiter at the big hotel. That is where you are staying?"

"That's right. I arrived last night."

"Spiro is waiter for long time," Niko told me, and I laughed, suddenly realizing why there seemed something so familiar about Niko's wide grin.

"I think I know your brother. I must tell him tonight that I've met you—and Delphinia," I added hastily. "Did you, er, name her yourself?"

"She is pretty donkey. Is pretty name," Niko said simply, and looked at Delphinia with so much love in his big dark eyes that I felt a lump come to my throat.

"Where do you live, Niko?"

"Come. I will show you." Niko took me by the hand and led me along the path until we came to a tiny isolated cottage with faded, jade green shutters. It had a small bamboo hut next to it and this, Niko solemnly explained, was Delphinia's residence.

Niko's mother, wearing a black shawl, her face wrinkled like the faces of most peasant women in very hot countries, came to the door when she saw us and greeted me.

"*Kalimera.*" Polite, shy, curious, she looked me over and then insisted on bringing me simple refreshments—a glass of ice-cold water, some cheese and a few figs.

Somehow I guessed, even before she told me, that she was a widow, for there was an air of great poverty about her cottage, clean though it was.

"I met your young brother today," I told Spiro that evening. Simon, as I'd hoped, had joined me for dinner and I had just been telling him how I'd spent my day.

Spiro grinned, and I added, "I met Delphinia, too. Niko's very fond of her, isn't he?"

"She is the apple of his eye," Spiro agreed, laughing.

"Who on earth is Delphinia?" Simon asked.

"Spiro's brother's donkey," I said solemnly.

"A donkey called *Delphinia*?"

"Ah, but she's a very pretty donkey," I protested, thinking that when Simon laughed he looked at least ten years younger. "I'm going to be allowed to ride her one day. Niko has promised to take me to somewhere called the Valley of the Butterflies."

Simon looked at me. Then unexpectedly he said, "Well, if you've changed your mind about having company . . . I didn't go to Knossos today after all, Sally. Will you come with me tomorrow?"

For a moment I caught my breath. Then I nodded. "Yes, I'd like to very much, Simon."

He wouldn't have asked me again unless he really wanted my company, I told myself. It would be silly to refuse when Knossos was one of the places I wanted to visit.

I found it breathtaking. Archeological sites can be pretty boring, but Knossos was very carefully restored by its excavator, Sir Arthur Evans. Simon and I spent all day wandering among the ruins of this most famous Minoan palace, and then instead of going back to the hotel for dinner, we found a little *taverna* where the smiling proprietor prepared us a simple meal of *dolmades*—stuffed vine leaves.

"This is the kind of place I would like to stay at," I said wistfully, and Simon nodded.

"Me, too. I loathe big hotels."

I looked at him in astonishment. "You do? Then why—I mean, you don't have a mother to get in a flap about drains and drinking water! Why didn't you choose somewhere like this?"

A dull red crept up beneath Simon's tan, and for the first time since I'd known him I saw him look discomfited.

"Oh, you know how it is! I took the easy way out," he said vaguely.

I didn't think it was a particularly satisfactory answer, but I didn't bother to argue. I was feeling far too happy and content. Today, I thought in surprise, I hadn't thought about Philip once. And I certainly no longer wished he was here.

I suppose I must be pretty stupid, but it was several days before I stumbled on the fact that the reason I wasn't missing Philip was because I was seeing so much of Simon. And that the way I was beginning to feel about the latter spelled disaster, if not for him, then certainly for me. Simon didn't care about me. He never had. That was why he hadn't minded when I'd left him to go to London.

I panicked. There's no other word for it. I couldn't bear the thought of being hurt again, especially as I had a horrible feeling that if ever I fell in love with Simon, then it wouldn't take me just a few months to forget him. It would probably take me the rest of my life.

"I'm sorry, Simon. I can't go out with you today," I told him firmly when toward the end of my first week on the island he suggested taking me to Phaestos, the ruins of another Minoan palace. "I'm going to ask Niko to take me to the Valley of the Butterflies. I did promise him, you know."

I didn't suggest that Simon might like to accompany us, and he didn't ask. He simply nodded, his face wearing a shuttered look so that I couldn't tell whether he minded or not.

There was no sign of Niko or his mother when I arrived at the cottage, but as I raised my hand to tap on the half-open door, I suddenly heard the sound of muffled sobbing. For a moment I hesitated, then very gently I pushed the door open a little farther. Niko was lying in a huddled heap on the floor, his head pillowed on his thin arms, crying his heart out.

"Niko!" Horrified, I knelt down beside him, "Niko! Why are you crying? What's the matter? I came to ask you if you and Delphinia would take me to the Valley of the Butterflies."

Niko raised his head, and choking back his sobs, looked at me with such misery and despair that I felt my blood run cold.

"I am sorry. Delphinia cannot take you anywhere. She is sick—very sick. My mother says she will probably die."

I caught my breath in dismay. "Niko, no! There must be something you can do to save her!"

"I bought her some medicine, but now it has all gone. Anyway, it didn't do her any good. She just got worse," Niko said dully.

"I don't suppose it was the right medicine. Niko, you need a vet—I mean, someone who knows all about sick animals . . ." I began, but Niko shook his head hopelessly.

"There is no money to pay him or to pay for more medicine. Spiro gave me all the money he had, every penny, but now he has no more, and my mother says he must not borrow."

So that was why Spiro had been looking so worried. Simon and I had both noticed his unusual air of gloom, but had not liked to remark upon it to him.

I rose resolutely to my feet. "Well, I know someone who may be able to help Delphinia, Niko, and it won't cost you a single drachma, so you needn't worry about that." Then as he looked at me with sudden hope, I said, "Wait here. I'll be as quick as I can."

My one fear was that Simon would already have left the hotel, but my luck was holding—I met him coming down the steps.

"Simon! Oh, Simon!" I caught hold of his arm and in a few breathless sentences told him the story of Delphinia's illness. "Can you help?" I asked anxiously. "I know you're on holiday, but poor little Niko—it will break his heart if anything happens to his beloved donkey."

Simon didn't waste time on words. "I'll have a look at her. There may be something I can do," he said briefly.

Delphinia was certainly a very sick little donkey. I looked anxiously at Simon as he bent over her, for almost overnight, it seemed, she had wasted away to nothing. Every rib showed; the once glossy hide was dull and brittle.

Simon asked Niko a few crisp questions and the child answered with almost painful eagerness. I could see that already he trusted Simon and would do anything he was told.

"It's an infection—pretty bad, but I think she's got a chance," Simon said to me. "I'll have to go into Heraklion to get the stuff I need, though. Will you stay here until I get back?"

I nodded. "Of course."

When he'd gone I put my arm comfortingly around Niko's shoulders. "He'll do the best he can, Niko. I'm sure if anyone can save your donkey, it's Simon."

Niko nodded, and together we waited with Delphinia until Simon came back from Heraklion. He gave the donkey an injection, then turned to Niko.

"This treatment has to be repeated every six hours, I'm afraid, Niko, so I'll be back again very soon."

"The *kyria*, too?" Niko asked.

I answered him firmly. "Yes, I'll come, too."

Simon looked at me. "That isn't necessary, you know, Sally. You stopped being my assistant a long time ago," he reminded me. I felt something prick the back of my eyelids as I remembered those happy months I'd spent with Simon.

"I know. I just want to come with you," I said gruffly.

By nightfall even Simon seemed a little happier about Delphinia's condition.

"A couple of more shots and if she responds to those as well as she has to these first two, she should be out of the woods," he told me. And then smiling at Niko, he said, "You can go to bed as usual, if you like, Niko. If you hear footsteps around about midnight, don't worry—it'll only be me coming to give Delphinia another injection."

"Me, I shall be awake," Niko said quickly, but since Simon and I both guessed how little sleep he had had the last two nights, we were not surprised when we arrived at the cottage just after twelve to find everything in darkness. Simon had a flashlight, and armed with this we crept into Delphinia's tiny dwelling. She made a faint snickering sound, and we could see that already she looked brighter.

I sat down on a pile of sweet-scented hay while Simon gave her the injection. I could hear his voice murmuring soothing words and with a sigh I closed my eyes. I swear it was only for a moment, yet the next thing I knew Simon was gently shaking me awake.

"Come on, sleepy head! Delphinia's all right. It's time to get back to the hotel," he told me, and pulled me to my feet.

I yawned and leaned against him. "Isn't it a good thing we're staying in the same place? Just think, Simon, if you'd picked another hotel we might never have bumped into each other again."

There was a moment's silence. Then Simon's voice, sounding oddly constrained, came to me out of the darkness. "Do you believe in coincidences, Sally?"

I was puzzled. "Well, of course. Don't you?"

"Not if you're referring to this one. I have a confession to make, Sally. I—I knew exactly where you were staying. That's why I decided to stay there, too."

I gasped. "You knew? But—"

"I met your mother one day and she told me not only that you'd broken your engagement, but that you'd decided to go to Crete for your holiday." Simon's voice became suddenly husky. "I just couldn't pass up the chance to see you again. I'd lost you once by being too slow and cautious."

"Simon! You don't mean—"

"I mean that I've been in love with you practically from the first moment I saw you!" Simon said roughly, and I sighed. Then in the darkness I put up my hand and with my forefinger I carefully traced the outline of his mouth.

"What did you tell me about thin lips, Simon?" I asked. "No emotion or enthusiasm, I think you said. Well, you certainly don't have thin lips, so—"

I left my sentence unfinished, but only because by that time I was in Simon's arms and I didn't have any breath left. Behind us, Delphinia whinnied. I like to think she was trying to show her gratitude by giving us gentle encouragement, but of course that wasn't in the least bit necessary.

We were managing very well indeed without it.

AUDRIE MANLEY-TUCKER

Honey for Tea

Every weekend Geoff and I drove down to the sea, where he had a boat moored. I crewed for him and became quite knowledgeable about the lean, haughty yachts that skimmed, white sailed, over seas that made me feel frankly queasy. I wasn't an enthusiastic sailor, but I hid that fact as well as I could because I was in love with Geoff.

Boats were his first love. I accepted that. He was patient and kind with me—until the time when we were coming in first in the yearly club regatta, and I fell into the sea.

From that moment nothing seemed to go right. I had the uneasy feeling that my handsome weekend sailor was about to walk quietly out of my life. It was time to suggest a change of scene.

"Why don't we spend a weekend in the country?" I said brightly. "We could stay with my Great-Aunt Clementina. She lives in a picture-book cottage smothered with clematis, in a dreamy village. She's adorable—sweet and unworldly and a marvelous cook. I can't think why she never married. She has a green thumb and a flair for antiques. Have you ever slept in a four-poster bed?"

"No," said Geoff, looking bored.

Oh, well, maybe I had gone on a bit about the one close relative I had left in the world. My memories of Aunt Clementina and the cottage were more than a year old because I had been so involved with Geoff. But suddenly a weekend at Tollington Purvey, with or without Geoff, seemed the most wonderful thing in the world.

"You go," he said a shade too eagerly. "It'll do you good."

"I have two weeks' holiday coming up," I told him.

"You need a complete break," he pointed out.

I know when I'm defeated. Perhaps absence would make the heart grow fonder—Geoff had said he was going to be very busy working on the boat.

I telephoned Aunt Clementina and asked her if I could come; she didn't sound her usual relaxed self. I thought she seemed harassed. How could she be? Since she had retired three years previously, she had done no more than putter in her garden, change library books or sit painting at her easel. On the one occasion that I stayed at Clematis Cottage, we had gone for long walks; I had soaked up the Rip Van Winkle atmosphere with great enjoyment.

Now she cried, "Sally? Darling, yes, of course, please do come. I need a spare pair of hands!"

It wasn't quite what I had in mind—being a spare pair of hands. I had thought of being spoiled, Aunt Clementina bringing me breakfast trays, listening sympathetically while I told her what a rotten sailor I was.

"Come as soon as you like, Sally. It will be lovely to see you. Life is a bit frantic, though I don't mind, really." She sounded happy. "I'll air the bed."

"What have you done?" I asked. "Got yourself heavily involved with the local jumble sale or fete or something?"

Her chuckle was wicked. "Oh, it's much worse than that," she cried. "See you. I must fly."

I puzzled over her words as I drove down to Tollington Purvey, out of the noise and dust of London. I arrived at the village late on a golden summer afternoon, and it didn't seem to have changed much since my previous visit. I drove past the old church, knee-deep in tall grasses and sunken tombstones; I saw the same straggle of cottages washed in sugar-candy colors and with patchwork aprons of flowers. There were little bow-fronted shops I remembered, plus a new pottery shop that I hadn't seen before. The only other changes were a bright new service station with a couple of pumps outside—and the loss of Rose Cottage Tearoom.

The tearoom had given character to the village, with rustic tables and chairs set out on the lawn on a summer afternoon. Aunt Clementina had taken me to sample their marvelous cream cakes.

Nevertheless, I sighed with pure pleasure, feeling a little less emotionally sore and bruised about Geoff. I thought of the peace I was about to sample; of my aunt's cottage, its big larder filled with row upon row of pots of honey and homemade jam. She probably had a chicken in the oven, turning golden brown ready for supper. There would be bowls of flowers everywhere, and Aunt Clementina would be sitting on the big window seat, watching for my arrival.

Her cottage was elegantly Georgian, like the one adjoining it that had been empty on my previous visit; both cottages had long sash windows and big front gardens; both had clematis covering their front walls in a green and purple shawl. I rounded a bend and came upon the two cottages; they were not as I remembered them.

The once empty cottage had its doors and windows wide open, revealing oak tables and chairs inside; its rather indifferent lawn had been made into a small parking lot. The hedge between the two cottages had been removed; on Aunt Clementina's side was the same smooth green lawn I remembered, the same willow tree, the same well-tended flower beds—plus a scattering of rustic tables and chairs that I instantly recognized. Over the porch was a large sign that said, Clematis Cottage Tearooms.

The tables had striped umbrellas over them to ward off the bright sun, and every table was occupied. A girl came through the front entrance carrying a loaded tray. She wore a long print dress with a ruffled white apron over it—very becoming with her long red hair.

"Does Miss Clementina James live here?" I asked helplessly.

"Tina? Oh, yes. Are you her niece?" the girl asked brightly.

"Yes," I floundered. "I'm Sally James."

"She's expecting you. Go straight into the kitchen. She'll be pleased you're here—tomorrow is my last day. I'm getting married next week, and the girl who is replacing me can't start for a few days."

I took a long, steadying breath and stepped inside the cottage. What had once been Aunt Clementina's dining room was now a tearoom; along the cream-washed walls were shelves with a miscellany of teapots in all shapes, sizes and patterns. The last time I had seen them they had adorned a Welsh dresser inside the Rose Cottage Tearoom.

I went through the swinging doors at the far end of the

tearoom. Inside was the kitchen just as I remembered it—bright, airy, compact. A woman was setting out tea trays with scones and jam and cream and some very delectable-looking homemade cakes.

As soon as she saw me, she smiled delightedly, came across and kissed me. "Sally, my love, how are you? The bed is aired, and we close in an hour's time. After that, we'll have a chat and a meal."

I looked at her accusingly. This wasn't my dreamy, unworldly Clementina who had always reminded me of that line from one of Rupert Brooke's poems, "And is there honey still for tea?"

This was a groomed and elegant woman who looked no more than fifty, who had slimmed away curves and wore smooth, blue-rinsed hair in a very attractive, flipped-up style; whose lips, like her nails, were rose tinted; who wore navy blue trousers and a crisp red and white top.

She saw my look and nodded happily. "It's all because of Mr. Tomlinson!" she assured me.

"Mr. Tomlinson?" I looked sharply at her hands, but they were bare of rings.

She saw the look and laughed again. "Oh, no, dear, nothing like that! He gave me moral support. The Rose Cottage people emigrated to New Zealand and everything was up for sale; the place next door to this was up for sale, too, so he said why didn't I do something as I was still a young woman. It was the right moment, he said. You know, darling, I always did rather fancy running a tearoom."

"You'd retired!" I cried. "You liked it!"

"True, dear. At first. It was such a nice change from running an office. Then I began to get so bored painting pictures and growing flowers and reading good books. So I gave my paints and brushes to Mr. Tomlinson's niece. . . ."

I began to dislike Mr. Tomlinson very much.

"You didn't tell me anything about all this," I said, still accusing.

Her smile was warm and carefree. "Oh, dear, didn't I? Well, maybe I wanted it to be a surprise. I knew you would be down for a weekend sooner or later. . . ."

Sooner or later. I felt guilty, thinking of the six-month interval, with only a couple of scrawls and a phone call or two from me. I thought of Geoff suddenly and wondered what he was doing.

"I'll tell Harriet to put a tray of tea in the lounge for you," said Aunt Clementina. No. Aunt Tina. The abbreviation suited the new image very well.

I went up to my room. There was the same high bed with the patchwork quilt and one of Aunt Tina's watercolors on the wall. She had filled a brown stone pitcher with garden flowers and left a pile of magazines on the window seat.

I changed into a clean gingham shirt, brushed my hair and looked at myself thoughtfully in the mirror. I saw a skinny girl with long brown hair and a rather subdued look on her face. I was thinking that I could scarcely expect Aunt Tina to take time out to carry up breakfast trays, and she wasn't going to have time, either, to listen while I told her about Geoff.

The big, comfortable room overlooking the patio and the back garden had an air of normality about it, but I could hear sounds of clattering crockery coming from the kitchen. I finished my tea, went into the kitchen and unhitched the apron from its peg behind the door.

"Aren't you awfully tired, darling?" Aunt Tina said, concerned but hopeful.

"Not really," I lied.

Promptly at six, Harriet went home and Aunt Tina and I finished the chores. A great, peaceful silence washed through the house.

"There's cold chicken and salad for supper," Aunt Tina said. "Mr. Tomlinson was going to come around to discuss the plans for the new kitchen extension next door, but he decided we might like an evening to ourselves, so he's coming tomorrow instead."

"That's nice of him," I said shortly. "What is he? An architect?"

"Oh, no, dear. He and his brother own the new service station in the village. I can't tell you what a help he has been to me."

I made a mental picture of him: sprightly, middle-aged, with an eye on Aunt Tina as well as on a thriving little business.

"He's coming to supper tomorrow evening," Aunt Tina added. "It's our busy day, Saturday. Plenty of people stop by on their way back from looking at the church or calling in at the pottery. What I'm going to do next week, until Harriet's replacement arrives, heaven knows."

I looked her straight in the eye, and she had the grace to blush.

"I can carry a tray," I said.

"You're a good girl, Sally. By the way, what happened to that young man who had a boat?"

I told her—briefly. She shook her head. "You never were much of a sailor, dear. Do you remember when you were twelve, and we took that steamer trip down the Thames from Westminster to Richmond? It was a summer day, flat calm, and you were sick."

I thought, forlornly, about her remark as I lay in bed that evening. I wondered what Geoff was doing and whether he was missing me half as much as I was missing him. I no longer believed the bit about absence making the heart grow fonder.

The next day I put on the long print dress I had intended to wear for lazy suppers at Clematis Cottage. Harriet loaned me an apron. I looked in the mirror and decided that the outfit was a distinct improvement on the jeans, shirt and canvas shoes that had been my weekend uniform for a long time.

Nevertheless, I was nervous taking orders, carrying loaded trays. Harriet was encouraging. Aunt Tina said I was doing very well.

"I'm closed on Mondays," she said. "We'll have a day out, dear. I want to try the new car."

I blinked at her, remembering the elderly, snub-nosed Morris that had been her pride and joy for so many years. "Whatever happened to Minerva?" I asked.

"I pensioned her off. After twenty years she had earned retirement. Besides, I wanted something a bit sporty. Mr. Tomlinson found me a last year's model, very reasonably priced, and of course, he can service it for me."

I counted up to ten and said nothing. He was coming to supper. I wanted very much to meet him.

Meanwhile, there were plenty of people wanting tea out on the lawn, because it was a lovely day. There was a lull around half-past four; clearing a table for two, I looked across to the front gate and saw a man standing there watching me.

He was tall and broad shouldered, with very thick, curly

brown hair. His mouth looked as though it was used to smiling a lot. I tried not to appear to be watching him. He pushed open the gate and walked across to the table I had just finished clearing.

"You're new," he said.

"Since yesterday," I told him. "I'm just a temporary. What's it to be?"

He gave me a wicked smile, his face full of shocked amusement. "What's it to be? You sound like Rosie, the barmaid at the Flagon of Cider."

"Sorry." I laughed. "I told you I'm a temporary waitress. I spend forty-nine weeks of the year in a publisher's office in London. I'm just doing this to help Aunt Tina."

He looked interested; he had very nice blue eyes and a suntan. It was a long time since I had noticed details about any man except Geoff.

"I'll have brown bread and butter," he told me. "Scones and chocolate cake. Oh, yes—and is there honey still for tea?"

It was strange. Quite uncanny, actually. As though there was some kind of rapport between us, which of course was ridiculous.

"I used to think of that particular quotation whenever I thought of Aunt Tina," I said.

He sat down, leaning his elbows companionably on the table. "And don't you think of it now?"

I shook my head. "She used to love pottering in her garden, reading, filling up her cupboards with homemade jam."

The wicked smile appeared again. "So now the customers get all the honey and jam, and you've lost your picture of a sweet little old lady," he said.

"Yes," I sighed. "She's enjoying it; and she's shed so many years I ought to feel pleased. It's just that there hasn't been time to get the new picture of her into focus. Besides, there's this Mr. Tomlinson."

I bit off the phrase too late. I had no business saying such things to a perfect stranger; but he looked kind and interested as though he really cared.

"Tell me about him," he suggested.

"I've never met him, but he's coming to supper tonight. He's responsible for what's happened to Aunt Tina. I think he pushed her into it. Made her discontented with her nice, peaceful retirement. He seems to have a great influence over her."

"He sounds sinister." The blue eyes sparkled. "What are you going to do about him?"

"Nothing," I admitted honestly. "What can I do? I don't like the sound of him, but it looks as though I'll have to start saving up for a wedding present."

He said nothing. I felt hot with embarrassment, wondering what on earth had possessed me to shed so much reserve simply on the strength of a shared liking for a certain line of poetry.

I scuttled indoors with my tray and exchanged it for one with clean china. I added buttered scones, thin brown bread, honey, and the chocolate cake that Aunt Tina always made so superbly—it was an old favorite of mine.

"You're a good girl, Sally," Aunt Tina said appreciatively. "If ever you're fed up with a typewriter, we could think about a partnership. After all, you're not the seagoing type, are you?"

I didn't answer.

He watched me as I walked toward the table, and he eyed the contents of the trays as though he hadn't eaten for days. "It's food for the gods," he said with a happy sigh. "I shall end up with a paunch."

I looked at his lean, hard figure and shook my head. "You're not the type," I told him.

He waved his hand toward the empty chair opposite his. "Join me?" he said hopefully. "It's not fun eating alone—I do it most of the time."

"Oh, I'll be fired if I fraternize with the customers," I replied lightly.

"That would be unfair dismissal." His face was solemn, but there was laughter in his eyes.

He was nice, I thought. His look, when he glanced at me, was interested. Geoff hadn't looked interested for ages—except when he eyed his boat. This stranger left me with a pleasant glow of warmth, and I wondered if he often came to the tearoom. I reflected that I had two whole weeks with Aunt Clementina, and then I dismissed both thoughts, trying to concentrate on the job at hand.

Alas, maybe I concentrated too hard. As I turned away

with what was meant to be a brisk and businesslike air, I trod on the frill of my long skirt. There was a tearing sound, and I measured my length on the grass.

He was on his feet in an instant. I was being helped gently to my feet, my arm held firmly in a tanned, masculine hand. "Now you'll *have* to sit down," he said with an air of authority. "Hot, sweet tea is the best thing for a shock."

I was glad to sit down. I was winded, my pride dented. Someone retrieved my tray and handed it to Harriet, who had come across to see what was wrong. The stranger opposite me smiled up at her and said calmly, "I'm treating her for shock. I'm sure you can manage without her for a little while."

Harriet laughed and her look made me feel foolish, but she murmured something about being quite able to cope, thank you.

I drank the tea slowly. My composure wouldn't come back, and I tried in vain to retrieve it. "It's no good trying to be a waitress in a long skirt," I said dejectedly.

"Nonsense. The Victorians managed very well. You look nice in a long skirt, anyway," he retorted.

"I'm more used to jeans," I told him.

"A pity," he murmured.

I finished the tea and stood up. "Thank you, Mr. . . ?"

"Christopher," he said. "Chris for short. Sure you won't stay and help me eat all this home cooking?"

I shook my head and murmured something about getting him a clean cup and saucer. In the kitchen Aunt Tina looked at me curiously. "Are you all right, dear? Harriet said you'd taken a tumble."

"So I did. A nice young man rescued me and gave me a cup of tea. Now that's real Walter Raleigh stuff," I told her, fixing the torn frill. "You know, Aunt Tina, I think I'm going to enjoy my spell as a waitress. It's fun. A change from the usual routine."

"Don't wear yourself out, dear. Remember, we have a supper date with Mr. Tomlinson."

I scowled at her. "He sounds bossy," I said.

She considered that remark, head on one side. "Bossy? No, I don't think so. He has a good brain and a clear-cut mind. Lots of people have such woolly minds, like unraveled knitting."

"Are you very fond of him?" I asked.

"Yes, dear," she said simply.

So that was it, I thought. Aunt Tina and Mr. Tomlinson. She certainly wasn't going to need me as a partner. I tried to look suitably pleased for her, but try as I would, I couldn't like this mysterious man who figured so largely in her life. Maybe it was because I still suspected his motives.

I carried out a clean cup and saucer to Chris. His smile was sympathetic. "How do you feel?" he asked.

"Fine. The shock treatment worked very well," I told him.

A car loaded with people turned into the little parking lot. I saw Chris look disappointed and thoughtful. *Maybe he'll come again. I hope so. I like him. He doesn't look the kind who would be bossy and know everything.*

When the last cup was rinsed, the last tea towel hung out to dry, I went upstairs to shower and dress. I decided the aloof, dignified approach was the best one for Mr. Tomlinson. There was a dress of soft yellow voile that I had put into my case at the last minute. I added a shady hat garlanded with summer flowers in pastel colors, put on a wide enamel bracelet. I looked at myself searchingly in the mirror, thinking about Aunt Tina with her brand-new image and champagnelike zest for living. I sighed and determinedly wished her happiness. I made a mental resolve to try very hard to like the man who loomed so large on her horizon. I thought about Geoff. The thought of returning to London filled me with sudden dismay. That was absurd. I'd always liked being there. I was just feeling dismal because I had a shrewd suspicion that Geoff wasn't going to be around anymore.

I heard car tires scrunch over the gravel, footsteps below the window. Slowly I went downstairs thinking, *I should have tried to be a better sailor.*

It was a lovely, warm evening. Westward the sun was going home slowly, as though it didn't want to leave such a perfect day. There wasn't a breath of wind and somewhere a lawn mower hummed lazily in the distance.

Aunt Tina had put chairs and a little wrought-iron table on the patio. As I walked through the lounge, I tried not to think about middle-aged Casanovas who wound the innocent Clementinas of this world around their little fingers.

I heard the sound of his voice as I stepped onto the patio. I recognized it at once, just as I recognized the face of the man who came forward to meet me.

"Sally," said Aunt Tina blandly, "this is Christopher Tomlinson. I believe you met this afternoon. Harriet told me about it."

I looked her straight in the eye. Her face was as innocent as a baby's. Christopher Tomlinson was no more than twenty-five at the most, and she looked at him with the same affection that she showed toward me.

"Christopher is a partner with his brother in the new service station, Sally," Aunt Tina continued. "They've both been an enormous help—Chris, especially. I'll bring out the drinks."

She looked demurely at me and moved indoors with surprising speed. I sat on the nearest chair feeling foolish, remembering my conversation with Christopher.

"You *do* look pretty," he said quietly, "like an advertisement for the classiest kind of garden furniture."

"Mr. Tomlinson!" I said furiously.

"I kept telling your aunt to call me Chris," he replied, unabashed. "However people of her age aren't comfortable using Christian names. Don't look at me as though I'm some kind of ogre."

I said nothing. I remembered my conversation with him. He had known who I was as soon as I began talking to him. He had taken an unfair advantage.

"I'm sorry you don't like the sound of Mr. Tomlinson," he said calmly. "There's no need to think about saving up for a wedding present, though—at least not on your aunt's account."

I wasn't often lost for words. On this occasion, all I could do was to stare over his head at the evening sky and the quiet trees.

"Listen to me, Sally," he said with sudden crisp authority. "You're being thoroughly selfish if you feel cheated just because your aunt wanted something she could get her teeth into; we met at the Rose Cottage auction, and she said she was tired of doing the things that people of her age were expected to do. So I told her it was time she did something about changing her image, and right now was the best time. Next thing I knew, she had made a bid for all the china and the furniture; then she looked dazed, like someone who has swum so far out to sea that they've no idea how to get back to shore. I told her she'd made a fine beginning and asked if there was anything I could do to help. There was no one else around. I made that path a bit easier for her, but I didn't set her feet on it, if that's what you're thinking. Anyway, can't you see how happy she is? Good luck to her. No one's going to put *her* in a corner before she's ready."

All the time he was talking, I felt myself shrinking. I ended up feeling about two inches high. Then, reluctantly, I met his eyes and saw that he was smiling at me. I stopped shrinking. I even began to grow a little.

"She talked about you," he said. "You were all tied up with a man who had a boat, and she said it wouldn't work because you're no sailor."

"She's right," I said. "It didn't work."

Didn't—past tense. Suddenly I was glad. Christopher looked pleased. He stood up to take the tray of drinks from Aunt Tina.

"Don't work her too hard!" he said to her.

She looked indignant. "As if I would! Sally is on holiday!"

His smile was for me as he answered her. "I know. I'm planning to take up quite a lot of her free time," he said.

I sighed contentedly. If there's one thing I like, it's a man who knows what he wants.

FRANCES MELVIN

Summer with Meriel

As the cool blue days of spring slipped into the dry and dusty days of early summer, there was a typical English heat wave, and suddenly women went about sleeveless, men shouldered their jackets and at opening times more people than ever turned in through the portals of the Tudor Rose.

They went, naturally, in search of refreshment—but for the spirit as well as the flagging body. For The Tudor Rose could not be circumscribed by the mere name "inn," or even "hotel." Those people who knew it well knew that once they were over the threshold that so befitted the Royal Borough of Richmond upon Thames, and made their way through the cool darkness to the rear of the hotel, they were about to walk out to the garden of all their dreams.

So it seemed when Guy found it four days after he arrived back in England. A small Eden, south of Sheen. His eyes, parched by the Middle-Eastern sun, were quenched by the tumbling honeysuckle and blue lobelia pouring from big stone urns. His memories of violence and battle were still close, so he found peace in the sweet white alyssum cresting the old brick walls like snow, in the walls themselves, that shielded the garden on two sides and excluded the possibility of cars. And at the edge of the garden a grassy bank sloped down to a narrow curve of the Thames, meandering along from some rural paradise.

Guy was young, thirty, but when he'd returned to England he had felt ancient, weary and dry. He had lost weight, and people thought his leathery suntan was the result of an early holiday, if they thought of him at all. No one took a great deal of notice of a man who sat alone at a wrought-iron table in a corner of the garden.

He had been coming here for a week. He felt less old now, less dried up. He would sit with his frosted lager and watch with quiet pleasure how the garden never seemed to be too noisy or crowded, never crammed too tight with people desperately enjoying themselves to the time meted out by the sounding of a gong.

His news editor had been sympathetic. Guy had been surprised.

"Best thing you could do is take a holiday. Buy a ticket—St. Tropez, Southern Spain. Have a good time."

Guy was tired of planes, of foreign sun and alien tongues. "I'll just go home," he told his news editor. "I have a bit of clearing up to do."

The editor nodded. He knew that Trish had left him. What a welcome home for the poor bloke, he had thought, on top of all that fiasco. Guy was due for some leave, anyway.

But the news editor had been mistaken in thinking that time off work would help. Guy found out it meant sitting around the riverside apartment he had taken just a month before going abroad, and remembering things like the dinner with Trish sitting on wooden packing cases and seeing some of her things still in the apartment. Worn copies of favorite books, some cooking utensils, a string of jet beads that had fallen down the back of the dressing table.

She had come to stay in the apartment while he had been away, keeping it aired, she said, and thwarting the burglars. Trish with her bright red nails and tap-tapping heels; the executive lady in her air-cooled office with its tropical greenery; Trish who said "dahling" in such a way and who hadn't loved him after all, in spite of her earnest promises.

Guy knew the pitfalls of this type of thinking, and he wasn't a man with double standards. He hadn't seen Trish more than twice in the last six months. Their on-off romance of three years had consisted of long times spent apart, and he couldn't blame her for not wanting any of that. It was simply that it was odd, uncomfortable, sitting around and thinking of her with her advertising man in Acapulco or wherever it was they'd gone for their honeymoon.

So he had gone out walking along the towpath to where the river curved in an arc and the path forked into some woods. And he came out alongside the water when he could, and one day he found The Tudor Rose.

After a while he noticed regulars in the pub garden and watched them carefully, not too long in case they should become aware and offended. He found himself most frequently drawn to one group of young people who came in most nights. They were bright and attractive and full of fun, but not rowdy, in their mid twenties, he would say.

Snatches of their conversation reached him and made him smile; they were always out to be amusing, and really they were quite droll sometimes. One night they were talking about a girl. He heard them saying "she" and "looking better," and many times they glanced at their watches and then at the French windows of the hotel that led straight out into the garden.

Later that night when it was dark and electric lamps shone on the stone urns and dappled the river, there was a cry of delight and a spatter of applause from the table. Involuntarily Guy's glance flew to the bright doorway of the hotel. A few other customers turned and raised their eyebrows and commented.

There stood one of the men who was usually with the group; in his arms he carried a girl who had her arms clasped about his neck. She withdrew one hand and waved; her eyes were dancing, and she had long, curly dark hair. The skirt of her dress hung down elegantly in a fan shape in front of the man.

He carried her to the table and set her down at the seat that had been pulled up by the others, and Guy saw then that the cumbersome object the man had had gripped under his arm was a pair of crutches. *They belong to the girl,* thought Guy. *She can't walk.*

Momentarily he was aware of a sickening reminder. There was a blinding flash of fire, he felt the impact, then he was in the dark and hearing a voice crying painfully for help.

He blinked his eyes and shook his head. Voices bubbled and people jostled all around him. These intruding flashbacks happened now and again.

Nobody, it seemed, had ever heard of Abin Hafar. Guy had been two months in Rawalpindi, then Lahore and Delhi, and was due to go home when the wire arrived. There were some military stirrings in Abin Hafar, and would he stop off there because Harry Nichols was in Africa? Harry Nichols was a war correspondent for the newspaper; Guy was one of its many foreign correspondents. He had been writing a series of features on the Brahamanic influence in contemporary Eastern life. At the Delhi Press Club they pulled his leg.

"Abin how-much? I should put in a complaint, old man. You're far too big for a page-five story like that."

"Three camels and a courthouse, that's the place."

Guy himself was exasperated and infuriated by the cable. "Look at it. I mean, it really says stop off on your way back. Stop off! It's a thousand miles out of my way."

A thousand miles and a week late for Trish, all because of some desert-bound little dominion that was only getting into the English papers because a number of Britons were living there, engaged mainly in engineering. Guy said a heavy farewell to the boys at the Delhi Press Club, boarded a plane and left India.

The airport at Abin Hafar's capital was just about big enough to land the jet he traveled in, although for a moment it looked as though the plane would overshoot the runway and roll smack into a row of stunted palms.

He took his belongings and checked into a hotel and called one of his contacts, a youngish-sounding chap called Hamid, who ran a newspaper of sorts. The streets looked remarkably normal for a city that was supposed to be facing a coup d'etat—people careering about on bicycles or in old German cars, sending up clouds of sandy dust. Guy found they spoke a language that was part Arabic, part something he'd never heard of, and his pockets were still full of rupees and he wondered if he'd been sent on a wild-goose chase.

He set off to see his contact, who spoke English. He was mildly taken aback at being stopped and searched on the way by a native soldier. There was a barricade across the street. He was allowed through. He found Hamid worried but optimistic; of course, this had been brewing for a long time; the cost of living had trebled and the unemployment situation had got worse, so what could one expect? The English people would be safe, of course.

Guy wrote to Trish. "I'll be back by the end of the week. Nothing is happening here and when I see old Crossley, I'll fix him."

But at the end of the week there had been a military take-over; there was a curfew, a halt of all broadcasting save that in use by the militia and a pile of rubble where Hamid's newspaper had been. Hamid was married and had one child, and was philosophical about the sudden obliteration of his livelihood. He would start afresh; there might even be better scope under a new leadership. He invited Guy to leave his hotel and come to stay at his home.

One afternoon a Royal Air Force jet was allowed to land at the airport and take away the British. Guy contrived to see the crew. "Will you take this home and mail it for me as a favor? Heaven knows what the mail is like from here."

The blue-uniformed officer took the envelope. "Letter to the wife?"

Guy shook his head. "Copy for the newspaper. And demands. I want them to get me out of here fast and get a war correspondent in. I'm a confirmed coward."

The officer smiled. "I'll be back in no time," he said unconvincingly.

"I don't suppose you'd post this as well?" asked Guy, pushing his luck. "To my girl friend. I wouldn't ask, but heaven only knows when I'll see her."

The officer agreed. "We're sending in a stork kite tomorrow," he said. Guy was baffled. These R.A.F. fellows still used jargon. Who else would call a plane a kite?

"A what?" Guy asked.

"Stork kite, pal. Complete with doctor, two midwives and a couple of dishy nurses. For the safe removal of all the pregnant moms."

Guy smiled. "I never thought of that."

The officer shrugged his shoulders. "Good job we do, eh?"

The next day the new government allowed the "stork kite" through, and the last of the emigrant Britons left Abin Hafar. A few stayed behind. The newspaper never did send Harry Nichols in and Guy stayed on to report, growing involved in the complexities of right and wrong, and growing an affection for the large-eyed, sallow-skinned people. The state was divided in two. The military seemed merciless;

the people pitted themselves constantly and even foolishly against them, and Guy found himself with fluctuating loyalties. He had never seen war before.

Hamid's wife and child were killed in a street riot. Guy was there when it happened. The shock peeled not only the scales from his eyes but impartiality from his senses, and from then on Guy's war became personal. Hamid seemed to take it stoically enough, but his optimism and his philosophizing were crushed. Guy confounded himself for his inadequacy. He wrote a special piece on Hamid's family, singling them out as "typical victims of a cruel and ruthless system," and it made a big impression on England. His telephoned report even succeeded in being recorded for the television news. All Guy knew was that sometimes when he looked at Hamid he saw a level of suffering in the man's eyes that had never come within Guy's reach.

In the garden of The Tudor Rose, Guy finished his lager and ordered another. The glass was slim, tall and icy cold. He sometimes felt he never wanted to stop drinking iced drinks, because he'd had them in his mind for so long. He took a long swallow, then put the glass back on the table.

The group with the girl were in high spirits, probably because she was with them. She must have been in hospital. He was home now, of course, and people were injured in everyday accidents, like car smashes or falling down the stairs. They were listening to her as she talked, and it seemed her conversation was witty, for they laughed often.

She was a lovely girl. He thought of "pretty" and "beautiful," but neither of those adjectives applied. Even from here he sensed a depth in her eyes and appreciated the generous warmth of her smile. There was something else about her, too, that he couldn't pin down. She would probably live to be a hundred-and-four years old and even when she was a white-haired wrinkled old lady, an inner beauty would shine through, and she would be wise and true and all her grandchildren would flock to her in despair when their parents didn't understand them.

She sat at the table in her long dress and was the distillate of all that was soft and gentle and yielding, all that he had forgotten about while in Abin Hafar. She held court, without reigning, and he began to watch her through the rosiest of spectacles, knowing quite well what he was doing.

The next day he walked by the sparkling river and in the hot afternoon sought the coolness of his riverside apartment and began painting the sitting-room walls. He'd had it on his mind to do this ever since he got back, but the farthest he had got was herding his furniture toward the center of the room and taking the blinds down. Now he enjoyed being busy.

That night after a light meal in a Richmond restaurant, he made his way to The Tudor Rose. He tried to stop himself from feeling an extra lightness of heart, a hopeful happiness that the girl would be there.

"The usual, sir?" The barman surprised him; he didn't normally speak. "Hot one today, sir, eh?"

Guy agreed it was hot, and that they'd best make the most of it, though it didn't suit some, and debated England's chance in the test match. He felt more like his old gregarious self tonight, but he was glad to prize himself away from the barman when other customers came in. He walked with his cold lager through the lounge, out the French windows and into the sweet, sun-filled garden. And there she was.

Guy did not know how tired he still was from his harrowing four-month stay in Abin Hafar. All he knew was that sitting here night after night in a charming English garden, with no obligation to be urbane or amusing, no one asking him impossible questions about the politics of the Middle East, his body began to unwind. Between his shoulder blades was an easing off of tension; his dark eyes in his weathered face began to observe rather than watch.

He observed the girl. In the light, early part of the evening he could see her better. The same man set her down and propped the crutches up against the wall. Her dark hair had streaks of gold, probably from much time spent recuperating, lying in the sun. Her face had a healthy glow; her figure was rounded and curvy. Womanly, he thought. Nothing like the skinny, tiny-waisted skeleton that Trish had constantly dieted for and talked of in a neurotic, rather defensive way.

He sighed and drew his hand across his eyes, and she was still there. He took a sip of his lager to hide his smile. Relief. He felt a great sense of relief.

The days developed an easy, contented pattern; he put in

more work on the sitting room, which was beginning to look good now; sanding down the bookshelves to give them a coat of gloss; getting occasional phone calls from friends and using the decorating as an excuse to turn down their invitations.

"But you'll have to come over when the place is finished," he told them. "There's a paved area outside the kitchen that could just conceivably be called a patio!"

As the light softened to early evening he would take a shower, change into light trousers and shirt, and after supper wander along to The Tudor Rose. Always he would try to discount or ignore a mounting buoyancy at the prospect of seeing the girl again. Always he would fail, and he would be looking in the direction of the garden before he'd moved away from the bar, anxious that she would be there.

Sometimes he couldn't get his corner table, and he would sit on a low wall that edged part of the grassy bank. A soft evening breeze would drift over the curving river, green and moist scented. How he loved England!

And slowly, gradually, he fell in love with the girl.

It was impossible for him not to; he never spoke to her, nor was he sure of her name. It was that kind of summer and it was just the right time in Guy's life to bestow on an unfamiliar young woman the qualities of feminine helplessness that he had never known in Trish. Just as the protective haven of The Tudor Rose garden had healed his disillusioned spirit on his return to England, so the sight of the girl in her long dresses, carried everywhere in the arms of her men friends, soothed his hurt pride because sophisticated Trish had upped and left him even before he came home. This, though, was a paradox. He began to invent a character around the girl, and nowhere in it was she incapable or silly or weak. Not knowing her or her friends was an ideal situation, for he could make her humorous (which she was, clearly, anyway) and tolerant, informed and interesting. She might live in a studio apartment situated, like his, on the river, and she might paint or be a concert pianist. Other times she lived in a renovated town house, was married to the man who most often carried her in, and had three imaginative children. She was strong because he could see she was strong, smiling over whatever discomfort her injury gave her, and friends probably confided in her—their marital problems and so on.

He almost didn't want to get close, to learn that she and her amusing circle of friends were petty or dull.

But Guy was only human, after all, and this vicarious existence had to come to an end. Fate works patiently on in the background and knows when too much distant speculation reaches a peak and collapses in mild boredom.

Some friends came to stay for two nights, and he didn't get down to his watering place. The next night he went there was hardly a soul in the garden, and noticeable by their absence was the group of lively young people who had been the focus of his attention. He was startled a little by the potency of his disappointment. Surely he was merely a watcher? Surely his main objective, recently, had been one of nonparticipation?

One of the regulars struck up a conversation with him: an elderly man who began with the test match, moved to the price of beer and the faults of the government. Guy liked the old man, who interspersed his talk with small, unintelligible jokes that he wheezed over. But after buying the old man a second drink, he left. He now felt frustrated for not knowing her name; there was no way of getting in touch, and he was sure he would never see her again.

In a way, he was right. He never did see that impeccable, silent, rather-too-unbelievable goddess girl again. But he did see Meriel. Funny, but out of all the exotic and enchanting names he had chosen for her, he would never have picked Meriel.

It came on the fourth day of not seeing her, the last day of the heat wave. Guy took a walk in the sultry afternoon and there was a heat haze so thick it smothered the horizon like purple down. Tonight or tomorrow it would rain, he thought. He was following the road that ran parallel to the river, and at last there was a flight of stone steps going down in terraces to the towpath. He started walking down the steps, hearing voices, muted and yet clear, floating on the still heat. A woman was standing to one side holding the iron handrail, not moving. Others passed up and down the stairway. She had walking sticks, but no long dress, and he knew it was her, even before he came alongside.

He paused. Hesitated. Then, "Want a hand?" he said.

She turned and seemed surprised. She looked at him and said, "I've seen you in The Tudor Rose."

Guy smiled awkwardly. He couldn't bring himself to echo her words. It would sound so phony. "Here, give me your sticks and if you take my arm—"

"No, no. That's very kind, but I must manage myself. Though—" she laughed ruefully "—I'd be grateful if you'd stay near me and make sure I don't fall."

She took a laborious step down, putting the weight of her body on the sticks. "Now that my cast is off," she said, mock mournfully, "no one wants to carry me anymore."

It took awhile to complete the descent. Long enough to exchange names. Did she live near here? "Yes, quite near. With my mother. She's a dressmaker and I'm her occasional apprentice." She stopped to rest and crinkled her eyes. "Maybe I'm a bit old for that."

So now she had a name, and a home and an ambiguous-sounding occupation. Guy found it incredible that he was helping her down to the towpath and then walking beside her, and that everything had changed. Close up she looked different and yet the same; her voice was quiet but clear, her eyes perhaps deeper. She was older, too.

They walked by the back gardens of cottages that ranged along this part of the river bank; roses climbed with languid, heavy heads and drooped over borders of yellow and red.

He didn't know what made him start talking about Abin Hafar, but once begun the details escaped from him little by little, and his mind's eye was far away. Meriel listened.

They stopped at last by a small house that she said was her mother's. It had a garden with a low wall, a trellis grown over with sweet peas and on the warm wall a sleeping bundle of fur that roused itself and stretched into the shape of a big ginger cat.

"Well." She leaned on the garden gate with one arm, and smiled at Guy. "Thank you."

He suspected that she was going to invite him in, and he would refuse because he had gone far enough in this dream without being disillusioned. It would be the end of all the things he had created for her.

He shrugged politely. "My pleasure. And, er, sorry if I rambled on too much about—"

"No." She shook her head. "You didn't ramble on."

The big ginger cat came stalking along the wall. It had a

gingery smudge on its nose. Guy liked cats. He started stroking under its chin and it purred noisily.

All was silent now. She, too, began stroking the cat, smiling a calm and secret smile. "This is Webster," she said, and put her face down close until her nose almost touched the sleepy-eyed cat's. "Give us a kiss, old Webster."

The back door to her house, Guy noticed, was at the end of the path, not open. Everything had changed and yet . . . .

Fate works conscientiously and life is not like dreams. Tonight it would rain, definitely it would rain, and the blurred edges would be washed away. More often than not it is better to watch the play and go home satisfied, in a mood of idle fantasy, than to take a part. But every now and then it is possible to come up close and not be disappointed, and then the scene is tantalizing, and truth can be beauty.

So it was for Meriel. Here he was, the man who had sat in the garden of The Tudor Rose, and whom she had seen one night looking at her in the way all women would like to be looked at just once in their lives.

It was a short step from the house in which Guy had never pictured her. He thought about it. Then he glanced at her, her face half hidden by an escaping fall of hair, one eye gleaming through the waves like a star. He thought he saw it, that intangible, elusive something he had sensed about her in the garden of The Tudor Rose. Then it was gone, chased away into the sunny afternoon, calling him to follow.

He laughed and shook his head. "You know, I thought—"

He had nearly told her what he had thought while watching her from a distance over those last many nights. It had been simple, as though he knew her well enough to say things like that. He would have to be careful.

"I thought this—heat wave would never end," he continued. "It'll rain tonight. We might have a good summer."

She turned her face up from the purring cat and almost said, "I know—we will," but caught herself just in time. She mustn't open up too soon, too easily. She must be very careful.

"Would you like to come in for tea?" she said.